A TIME FOR CHANGE

by

DeWitt C. Tremaine

Revised Version

ISBN: 978-1-966954-42-2 (paperback)
ISBN: 978-1-966954-43-9 (hardcover)
ISBN: 978-1-966954-44-6 (ebook)
Library of Congress Control Number: 2025910096

Printed in the United States of America

TABLE OF CONTENTS

Book Titles by

DeWitt C. Tremaine

Ethar World Series:

1. The Rise of a King – Book One of the Ethar World Series
2. A Time for Change - Book Two of the Ethar World Series
3. A Touch of Earth - Book Three of the Ethar World Series
4. Savage Continent - Book Four of the Ethar World Series
5. A Journey - Book Five of the Ethar World Series
6. Tallund - Book Six of the Ethar World Series
7. Telsa - Book Seven of the Ethar World Series
8. When Nothing Happens - Book Eight of the Ethar World Series
9. From Kendlar and Back Again – Book Nine in the Ethar World Series

Touch of Earth Saga:

1. Touch of Earth Saga 1 Heroes
2. Touch of Earth Saga 2 Secret Camp
3. Touch of Earth Saga 3 Janet
4. Touch of Earth Saga 4 Candy

CHAPTER 1

Shadows

"You be careful about what you are doing, you know it is not just a game anymore." Bonny had said.

"No worries love, I know what I am doing." The words of their earlier conversation nagged in the back of his mind.

Bright flashing arcs filled the air, each followed by its own booming crash of thunder. Eric mumbled to himself, he really did need to check things out in a little more detail before he exercised his powers of demigod-hood or the 'powers of the Ancients' as they so delicately put it on Ethar. Now he was working up a sweat protecting all the innocent little creatures from the storm he had just generated. His mind reaching out, he couldn't feel any more out there.

He had been granted a great deal of power passing through the barrier to Ethar the first time and inherited the powers of the Ancients and granted even more power by another dimensional barrier when he repaired a breach. He had since discovered that the powers he had traveled with him back to earth and to anywhere else he went for that matter. There had also been several boons he had granted, before he realized the fullness of what he had. His life had definitely changed after his first visit to Ethar with his little Eftite friend Shiheel. Jamis never did return to earth, rather kept his pseudo-name Hans Spardic and still lives on Ethar, though his life had become a lot more than just the weapons master after he left for the middle continents.

Eric had been reproved for a few of the boons he had granted. Gifting Hans the ability to morph into an extremely large hawk-like bird was one of those boons. He discovered shortly after that though he was not the only 'ancient' playing a strong hand in the events of Ethar. Hans called him to learn more about what it meant when the color of his blood had changed to white. Hans had moved into the town of ShadowKeep. There was also some question as to how restrictions on the older ancients may or may not apply to the new ones. There were only two 'new' ancients that they knew of, Eric and Bonny, but the fact that they were granted such great power opened up possibilities.

Shiheel who brought Eric through the barrier between dimensions using a mixture of science and magic did not know the changes he would go through. He did point out that it was predicted by the Never-ending Poem. From what Eric could see the Never-ending Poem was open to a lot of interpretation. There were enough verses that you could just go through and pick what you wanted to see as applying to an event.

The Eftites like Shiheel were also not native to Ethar. They came from the same dimension at least, but they had been from a different planet. They were a shorter race and they looked alien. The partial metallic looking exoskeleton and the three multifaceted crystalline eyes gave them the bug-like alien look. The extra knee in each leg and elbow in each arm and the tail that worked like a third arm or leg all contributed to the alien impression. They seemed to be a very considerate race who cared as much for others as they did themselves once you got to know them.

Having removed all the little creatures to safety Eric finished his experimenting, cleaned up and with a gesture stepped through the portal into his living room on earth. Bonny still worked at the hospital and he still worked with the university, though his game design had taken off on the Internet, a great success and was enough to justify any change in lifestyle they wanted to make. After talking it over the two of them had decided to give things time before they made any changes to their earth lives. Although not everything was easy to hide from everybody.

Bonny's mom had made a miraculous recovery, from being on her death bed to being healthier than she had been in years. She still gave Bonny a hard time about staying with a lazy lout like him but seemed to go out of her way to fix his favorite dishes and bring them over as a surprise on a regular basis. He could even smell her cooking as he stepped from the portal and it vanished. The smell summoned him to the kitchen.

"Oh, and there he is now, my favorite son-in-law." She cracked as he came into the kitchen.

"Your only son-in-law!" He smiled back. She had found out about their little secrets, but got lost in their explanation and just settled for knowing a little of what they could do, though when she spoke of it she referred to it as that "game stuff" you guys play.

"Knew I could pull you out of hiding if I brought some food over!" She gently wafted the smell of her spiced batter fried chicken in his direction with her hand.

Eric smiled, gave her a quick embrace of greeting and moved over to sit on the other side of Bonny at the dining room table, "It smells wonderful!" then with a smile and a wink, "So what are you extorting with this peace offering?"

"Eric!" Bonny interjected, "Be nice."

Eric reached over and picked up a cup of coffee that had not been there until he started reaching for it. "Yes, dear, wouldn't want to offend her and loose the inheritance." Mom feigned being offended for a moment and then they all laughed. Bonny passed them each a plate and started serving her mom's food while it was hot, batter-fried chicken, potato biscuits, and broccoli in cheese sauce in little bread cups, a full meal in finger foods. "You know you really should open a restaurant, Bes." Her full name was Elizabeth, but everyone that was close to her called her Bes.

"You kids could do that; I'll give you all my recipes. I have already retired." Bes smiled with all her grandmotherly charm, "That is as soon as you get married and give me a grand-kid." She added chuckling.

"Mom, now you know we have other things going on, you could hire anyone you wanted to run a restaurant for you. At the very least you can put together a recipe book and sell it." Bonny glanced at Eric and turned back to her mom, "As far as us getting married, you know we already are, and we intend to make it official here too and we did set a date, so relax already."

"Now kids, you may think it is 'OK' as long as you both feel the same way, but I am a little old fashion and will be happy when it is really official." She sat back and regained her composure, "Have you picked out invitations yet, Bonny?"

"Cost will not be an obstacle." Eric tossed in, "I want it to be your perfect wedding."

They chatted through dinner. When he finished eating Eric left them still discussing wedding plans as he went off to the computer in the office. Since they now shared the same bedroom he had to move the computer. He sat down and brought up the game screens. His game was spreading like wildfire across the nation and even internationally, but what he was interested in now was the divine requests data. The first thing he had to do was sort out what was from the game and those requests that were for him from Ethar. He took this task very seriously. Real lives hung at his fingertips and every decision he made could have an effect on the course of events of an entire world. He had already done more than his share of fumbling, but the other Ancients seem to take it all in stride. They even seemed to look to him for the course of events to come and yet they all knew a lot more than he did, at least he hoped they did.

Eric chuckled as he started reading down the list, time seemed to lose its relativity between dimensions, and no matter what situation he was dealing with, he knew whatever he needed to when it came to events on Ethar. Here on Earth, while he retained immortal powers from the other dimension, he did not have the same knowledge outside the normal means, at least not with events in his game world. He had not tried on Earth to step out of the normal bounds of time. He had learned how to compress and expand time on Ethar, and though he could see usefulness in expanding time, he had yet to find a practical use in compressing it. If he thought about it there was actually a lot, he had not tried to do, or experimented with on Earth. He really did not want to try experimenting with what he could do on Earth because at least a part of him did not want to change the rules that he had come to accept as the way things were.

The list was long as usual even though he allowed certain requests to be run through the divine intervention program he had set up for the game. He had learned the hard way what he could allow to be filtered that way and what was more important and required his personal attention. A harvest being a healthy harvest did not require his attention; it could be credited to the natural flow of events, whereas an abundant harvest to compensate for the fields lost to fire would require more evaluation of the situation. He had learned from that one to find out if one of the other Ancients was involved before making major changes.

Many requests were simply to watch over and protect families from harm, which became a real problem for him when wars broke out. Many were simply not genuine and for the most part they were dismissed. This was one of those occasions where he would stop time if he were on Ethar so he could respond to each at his leisure. At least everything he needed to know about each was still there and even if not, lightly he could make his decisions quickly. "The burdens of the ancients." he sighed to himself.

His game had taken off so big that they had purchased a building downtown to house the servers for the massive on-line support. Eric still kept servers and certain exclusive control over some divine intervention in his basement. The events on Ethar seemed to channel through his equipment which kept the people working at the downtown building from having access to information concerning Ethar.

A knock came from the front door. Bonny was already opening it as Eric walked up. "Good evening officer Terrell; come in. Can I get you something to drink?" Bonny ushered the officer in. "What brings you by this evening?"

Well, we still haven't solved the disappearance of Jaffro Jamis. He still has not been seen since that strange snowfall." The officer looked almost apologetic for bothering them again. "You folks still seem to be the last ones to have seen him."

"Maybe he got zapped into another dimension." Eric jeered before thinking about it. "Sorry officer, I know this isn't a laughing matter, it is just I have no better explanation for you and we have gone over all the details several times already. I really do not know the reasoning behind his disappearing." Though Eric knew Jaffro was Hans and had chosen to stay on Ethar, it was the truth that he did not know his reasoning in the matter.

"I know, and you folks have been more than generous in your cooperation," the officer sighed as he sat down at the kitchen table. "But the Chief wants me to check out all the details one more time."

Eric was thankful as he noted that Bes had already left. "It is your job." Eric said flatly in an understanding manner. "He was a good student." he added with all sincerity.

"Honestly, Mr. Marland, the Chief doesn't trust you and he is trying to find a motive. He thinks Jaffro might be dead and you had something to do with it. I told him he should come and talk to you himself. He insists on biding his time till you 'slip up.'"

"He should like that." Bonny commented casually.

*   *   *   *   *

Gaharias pondered his last conversation with Eric. Eric had asked, "Why did their blood turn white when they moved to Shadowkeep?"

"During the wars" Gaharias explained, "I sought a way to stop the advancing of the evil armies of vampires and undead. I placed a binding on land for all that made that their home, that they should be changed, and their blood should be poison killing any undead or creature of evil that should try to feed upon them."

"They were okay with this?" Eric asked, showing innocence that Gaharais had not expected.

"This new race, well not exactly race, but they were to bring an end to the war that was destroying the continent. No, I did not ask them. Perhaps I was wrong in not asking, it is a mistake that I have to frequently deal with still."

"Did it end the war? I mean if it worked, couldn't you just change them back?" Eric had seemed so matter of fact that Gaharias paused before answering.

"My son, perhaps generations removed, there are things that when done can have a very bad effects if you undo them. Yes, they did bring the wars to an end, but not as I had intended. They became a stopping point and a sanctuary, not the armies I hoped to push back the enemy with. I was younger and more foolish than I am now."

"How can it be bad to undo what you did." Eric had a look of concern.

"Well, look at the adoma you placed at the heart of the city of Talmorg. If you were to remove that life giving force now, all of the life and health that has sprung forth from it would begin to die. The land, the creatures, the people there would all suffer. The change I bound there pulled forces in a dimensional rift. If you go into the village within the circle of mountains, you will find it is bigger than can possibly fit. That village can grow as big as it needs to to accommodate anyone who chooses to live there. I cannot undo part of the binding without undoing the whole."

Understanding had entered Eric's eyes, "So if you undid the binding most of the village would be lost and many would suffer. You cannot undo it in part because it is all bound together." They had talked on about a few other matters.

Gaharias found he was pacing again and forced himself to stop and lean on the mantle of his fireplace. With a fleeting thought he started a fire in the hearth as he looked around the sparsely furnished room. Stepping across to the only chair in the room he sat down and stared into the flames, pulling a golden goblet filled with nectar out of the air. The Old Ones allowed Eric to have free course with his powers. They told Gaharias he should accept this, after all they knew a lot more than he did. It is like setting a child loose in a field of hay with a torch, he thought to himself.

The Old Ones had told Gaharias that Eric was subject to none of the restrictions that were placed on the rest of the Ancients. Eric was of Gaharias' family, but he was raised as a human. Eric was a descendant of the lost bloodline on earth. Eric's lineage was lost at the time of the separation of earth from Ethar, long before the Ancients were subject to any restrictions. Not only did Eric have all the powers of a full-fledged Ancient, he had the endorsement of several of the barriers. The barriers are the intelligent forces that hold existence together and dimensions apart. Gaharias knew Eric had more power than he did and wondered if the Old Ones were afraid of him and would not act to restrict his activity because Eric was more powerful than they were.

Gaharias looked at his own reflection in the golden goblet. "You have been the most powerful of all Ancients for a very long-time old friend. Tell me; are you really worried or just jealous of his seemingly limitless power?" He shook his head and took a long draw from his goblet. They had been in full control on Ethar once, and then the Old Ones told them they had to give the younger races a chance to grow and rule themselves. The Ancients should be as guardians to the younger races guiding and instructing them but giving them their own rule and destiny. Gaharias stared into the flames again, it was his brother that had led the revolt against the instruction of the Old Ones, and it was Gaharias that secured order. Although they had conspired together, Gaharias had assisted Darval in making his escape with the dark council in secret. He wondered if his brother might have been right. An itching came to his ears from the shadows in the flames. The voice of Darval struck his ears. It is not too late to try again, my brother. and faded as Gaharias considered the words.

Maybe they are afraid of Eric, Gaharias began to relax, perhaps we were pulled out of the affairs of the world before we reached our potential, and perhaps they are afraid of us. A tear formed in the corner of his eye as the battle began within him anew. He always stood for what was right, didn't he?

He heard the call and felt time stopped. He knew who was calling and stepped through.

*   *   *   *   *

Chareece was the firstborn to Saphrine, Talmorg was her daddy, her father was the legendary Eric of the Ancients and yet of earth. She walked with the wind a shadow and a free spirit. The most powerful of Ancients Gaharias could not even follow her or track her. She had taken on the title ShadowDancer and none other than a very few of the Ancients knew who ShadowDancer really was. Her father was one of those Ancients, who seemed always to look after her wellbeing when he wasn't preoccupied with the business of the Ancients or his other world or worlds. She often wondered about her father's other world, earth perhaps she would go there one day. Chareece knew all she had to do was ask and she could have her father's full attention. The blood of the Ancients raced through her veins and mix with the elf magic.

She had asked her father, Eric, how he could give her so much of his time. He had explained something about altering time, but she never really wanted to know. Chareece was just glad he had the time to give her. Chareece lived a life of an ordinary she-elf, well that is as ordinary as a king's firstborn daughter could live. She had learned to conceal the extent of the powers she had inherited and no one in the kingdom knew she was special in any way other than being the first princess among the children of Talmorg and Saphrine Elkinshane. She had also become quite practiced at slipping away unnoticed to live her alter-ego ShadowDancer, slipping around untraceable and hidden from those who might seek her out. Chareece learned that the few ancients who could locate her were all of the Emarlandestria lineage, the same bloodline she received from Eric Marland. They had a common blood and could sense their own.

Sleep was a rare thing for her and then only an hour or two when she did sleep even without practicing elf meditation. She had learned years ago how to get as much rest as she wanted in a moment of time, adjusting time she liked to call it, perhaps something like what her father had tried to explain. There were many methods she used to slip out unnoticed when others thought she was sleeping in her chambers. She had almost been caught once; it was Talmorg, her dad, making his occasional rounds randomly checking to be sure everything was well with his family. He was staring out the window when she slipped in. He was just sitting on the edge of her bed staring out the window. First, she had to convince him he just had not heard the door when she came in, and then that she had only gone for a stroll in the garden for several hours. After that happened, she started setting an enchantment on the room that dissuades any from entering and alerts her immediately if they do.

Chareece chuckled as she remembered the lecture on families and responsibility she had gotten after convincing him. He was a good dad and she wondered why she did not just trust him with her secrets as she faded into the shadows and slipped between the cracks in the door. The shadow form was the easiest way to get around without being seen, once in a while she would draw a glance in the direction she had passed, but then she was usually more careful than that.

She slipped quickly through the palace and out into the city, heading in almost a straight line for the location in the outer wall of the city. She had made a habit of passing through the same place in the wall. There was a group out there who had taken it upon themselves to start worshiping her and she was going to pay them a visit tonight. Their worship was most flattering though she still had not decided if she liked it or not. She felt energized, but also did not know if it was right, she was not officially considered an ancient, but her father was and he accepted certain amounts of worship, not that he had a choice. For an ancient her father Eric was not as lofty as the rest and never tried to project an image of being perfect just because he had more power.

Chareece had more power than her peers as far as she knew. She could do things only the Ancients were supposed to be able to do and she often wondered how much power it took to be considered an ancient. This only brought on another paradox in her mind, if she was an ancient would she have to leave her life with family and friends or would she have to give up her power to stay with them. No one had ever confronted her with this, so she was not going to bring it up either. It could be that no one else had thought about it or knew the power she had. For the time being she lived two lives.

ShadowDancer slipped out into the night air, letting the portal she had formed in the city wall close behind her. She had also learned more from the Eftites, Shiheel and Hesheil, than they were aware of, mixing the magic of one with the science of the other. Laughing as she faded into the shadows and stepped out on the wind, ShadowDancer was a mystery that drew a certain amount of respect anywhere in the world. She was heard of in places that even the Eftites had never traveled.

As she passed through the outer wall and vanished into the darkness, Chareece thought she felt someone watching her leave. In the dark and shadows, she transformed into ShadowDancer and turned to find the eyes that had watched her shadow form pass from the wall of the castle. Morning's light was radiating the glow that foreshadowed sunrise. There was nothing gave evidenced the eyes that she felt were anything more than paranoia. She only had a short time, not really satisfied with what her search showed her, with a thought she was looking instead upon a gathering in a distant meadow. There were several people she recognized, the assemblage was mostly half-bloods, a term that referred to mixed races and outcasts. She had helped most of them at least once, their crimes against those who would persecute them no more or less than the fact they were born of mixed races. Chareece considered herself to be of a mixed race, her father Eric was either human or ancient and her mother was High-Elf.

This small crowd was gathered to show her respect. They were not well organized and appeared to have no particular leader, but they all had in common praise for ShadowDancer the naked goddess. It seemed being outcasts of their races they chose not to show respect for the Ancients, but rather used the term the humans used to refer to her. ShadowDancer like the sound of goddess in her ear, from what she had learned humans had many levels of gods and goddesses. These seemed to range from those having a little more power than normal folks to those with endless power. She could accept that kind of elevated position, it actually was not that different from her role as princess. She slipped through the crowd unnoticed dancing from shadow to shadow, from what she picked up they were planning some great sacrifice in her honor.

As she approached the center of the crowd, she could see an altar that had been built in her name, and some self-appointed priest she did not recognize. ShadowDancer slipped into the shadow cast by the altar to observe the occasion.

"....and in the same manner we showed him our respects, we shall offer up to ShadowDancer a pure sacrifice. We shall show her our support and give her the strength of our souls that her power and influence might grow." ShadowDancer did not catch whose manner the priest was referring too, but he was well spoken and brought a raucous of support from the crowd. To her he felt out of place in this gathering, something was very wrong.

The flickering of the torches made it easy for her to remain hidden in the early twilight shadows. Three more cloaked figures approached the middle one shorter than the other two. ShadowDancer began to feel uncomfortable at their approach. The figure in the middle was a young human-elf halfling female barely old enough to be a woman and her face radiated with happy innocence. The figures on either side said something ShadowDancer did not hear as she started trembling within, but the girl's lovely voice cut straight to her heart.

"I give myself heart and soul to the service of my goddess." The young women caste off her robes and laid her naked form upon the altar, with a cheerfulness that made ShadowDancers anger boil at the abuse of her innocence. While she hesitated undecided what to do the figure leading the proceedings pulled a large Sacrificial blade tinged with a magic of its own high in the air above her and started lunging downward toward the young woman's heart.

Time stopped. "Father!!!!!!!!" The scream echoed in her head as her flaming shadows rose up through the altar. This was the first time her presence in the realm of the Ancients was felt. This was the day the power of ShadowDancer was awakened.

*   *   *   *   *

Hans Spardic looked out over the vast expanse of land in front of him. No one could approach Shadow Keep unnoticed and only one road wound its way up the baron rock face of the mountain. This was the home of the High Lord of the White and every member of the village hidden within the mountains took a turn keeping a part of the watch. The middle continents were a riddling of wars between lords and kings. Hans the Ebony Warrior, Weapons Master of Ethar felt quite at home in this environment defending a good people.

A long time ago he had played a game with a good friend, Eric. After he had decided to stay in the world of Ethar he learned that his friend became a "god" here, "Ancients" the title by which they are known. To him, it actually seemed fitting since he was a Game Master, which put him in the position of having power over everything in the game, not unlike a "god" or "ancient". Having become a character he used to play in the game with his friend, he requested the ability to fly, so that he could search the middle continents of this world to see if his characters parents lived there. This was important to him because in his prior identity before leaving earth he had never known his real parents, they died when he was too young to recall.

Eric granted his wish, but in order to fly he had to transform back and forth between being Hans and a giant hawk-like bird form. He developed an alternate identity known as RavenHawk. His darker skin was too rare in the northern continent to support an alternate identity. When he found the place where his "parents" were supposed to have lived, he discovered a field with not even two stones standing upon one another in memory of the village that he was sure had once been there. So, Hans like Jaffro had no family ties, not even a relic of his past.

Hans continued to explore the middle continents, bringing Stralina the Jinn with him on his journeys here and back to the training school he had opened to the north in the years past. They eventually decided they wanted to live in the middle continents. After getting married, they bought a plot of land in Shadow Valley and settled into their new home. The village and High Lord all treated them as family, and it was easier here to maintain the secrecy of his alternate identity of RavenHawk.

They seemed to be settling into their new life without a hitch, until one day while sharpening one of his blades he put a small slice in his thumb. He would not have thought anything of it except his blood was white and ate right through the metal of his blade. That was when he learned that the ancient Gaharias had bestowed strange working upon the village. The villagers knew some of it and the rest he found out from Eric. This was one of the times Eric actually got him considering a return visit to earth.

The village was a pawn being used to combat an upsurge in creatures born of darker powers. The white blood was poisonous to a wide range of creatures born of evil including Vampires and undead. None of them were pleased with being used as pawns by the Ancients, but they were one of the races, if you could call the transformation a race, that were up for grabs. For most their prior ancient had been a member of the dark council in the wars of the Ancients. It was one of the ancients that had vanished before the final defeat, eluding the ability of the ancients to know where each other are. To speak of the dark council was forbidden throughout most of Ethar, but rumors of their return and the rise of the powers of darkness were starting to become more common. Such things were foretold in the never-ending poem, the same poem that mentioned his arrival long before it had ever happened. He wondered if this was the source of the rumors, the poem mixed with idle time.

In the distance he could see the small cloud of dust rising from a slow-moving caravan coming their way. With his ability to transform into the giant birdlike form, he had gained excellent long distant vision and would be able to identify the approaching caravan before others were even be able to see it. He waited patiently until he could see it was a merchant caravan. He watched a little longer before turning to report the approach. Something was not quite right about what he saw, but he was having trouble putting a finger on it.

Maybe it was because the caravan though marked right for merchants, maintained more of the regimentation of a military escort. Hans shook his head; he would let the High Lord know his apprehensions also. The billows of dust seemed to stop moving. The sounds of the market below stopped. Time was frozen. He was caught in the moment. This was the working of the Ancients; at least one of them was calling him. He saw who and stepped toward the call, willing himself to answer.

*   *   *   *   *

Merlin Starnook sat in the study where he now lived in the Walled city of Talmorg. If he was right in his reading of the scrolls and the many verses of the never-ending poem he had acquired, the shadows of change had but barely begun. The Ancients surely must know that Darval will return, and the dark council will rise again. It is the coming of wars and darkness, he had begun preparing, but he was worried that the tranquil period peace and unity was causing some to lose caution.

Merlin looked out over the open markets, appreciating the social interaction of a civilized people. He watched the people milling about, dickering and bartering, and those debating issues in the political and social forums. It reminded him in some ways of the ancient Athens he had enjoyed visiting long ago.

The city of Talmorg indeed held a civilized people, something he had seen so often fall to greed and human frailty. Well, the frailty that can be found in any sentient emotional species, not just human, but the phrase fit. He could only hope that with the blending this city had, it could stay civilized longer than most. He had lived long and lost count of how many times he regained youth and grew old again. The shadows of things to come clouded his mind as he looked over the wondrous city.

He felt the tingling and suddenly everything seemed to freeze in place. The fly that had been buzzing in and out of his window stopped suspended in the air in front of him. Time had stopped and he was between the moments. Merlin knew the spell, he always had one ready at a moment's notice, but this was someone else and he was included from a distance. This was something new to try to figure out, but who with such power had included him, meaning to or not? The one thing he knew was this marked a turn of events; just what he would have to ferret out in the moment or when time started again. He heard the call, turned and headed towards her.

*   *   *   *   *

They had created a world in the twilight realm an abyss Darval Emarlandestria had discovered not long before their rejection from the world of Ethar. It was a hidden place that even the Old Ones did not know about. In a way the twilight realm did not really exist, perhaps the Dark Council brought it into being, bringing pieces of other realms to a place where there was nothing before. Everything that was in this place was of their making, even the rules that governed how things worked. It was the edge of chaos.

Darval had felt it when his keep had been resurrected on Ethar. He went slipping in and out following the flow of events, not with any real interest; it was no longer his world, no longer his concern. Though he did note that he is expected to try and return there at some time, he hoped to disappoint them. He had his own world and realm now; they had gathered from many other realms, taken of the rejects and created a new life. They had gathered lost souls and given them a new start. They had their own peoples and their own wars to deal with. There was no need to return accept to gather those followers he left behind with the promise of his return.

Suddenly in the middle of things as usual alone scream was heard across the multi-folds of existence and time was stopped around him. Who had the raw power to bring time to a stop even to a place that did not exist? He could feel the calling of a common blood. A plea without clear definition reached him. He would go and check this one out perhaps he was not done with Ethar as he had thought, but if not, he would have to be subtle. Darval decided he would take Count Morracon High Lord of the undead with him. There could be more to this game then he had previously thought.

*   *   *   *   *

Jahaln thought of himself more like a surviving scavenger than as an adventurer and perhaps there was a good deal of truth to the thought. He had set out on his journey of manhood some 23 years ago from his Milmorg village and simply never gotten around to returning. He had been scavenging and traveling with a wide range of different groups, though he had started learning a little more caution after the first adventure party he had joined.

As he trudged alone through the mountain forest he reflected back on that adventure. He had been invited to join a small group of adventurers who told him they were going find a buried treasure. What they failed to tell him was they had buried it after stealing it from a nearby dwarfish cave and they were setting him up to take the fall for them. After three weeks of incarcerated labor, the dwarfs decided he was too naive to be guilty, paid him three weeks wages and sent him on his way. He would have been happy with that, but the dwarfs somehow forgot to mention they were using him for bate to capture the real thieves. Getting a share of the recovered treasure overshadowed the three months medical care and bed rest and gave him his hunger for adventure.

Suddenly in mid-thought the ground gave out under Jahaln and snapped his mind back to the present. When he finally quit falling, the dust settled, and he realized he did not have any broken bones he looked around to assess his situation. Looking up he could see the late evening sky through the hole about thirty feet up. There was a breeze coming from the darkness in front of him with the smell of an old grave. It was not safe to try to get back out the way he came in, judging by the look of the walls around him, he was already lucky he had not buried himself.

With a flick of his wrist there was a small thud about ten feet in front of him and from that point a green glow lit his surroundings. What he saw appeared to be the remnant part of some ancient catacomb, still intact, well sort of considering even with the numerous cave-ins it still looked passable. The thought of ancient treasures and runic magic brought a smile to his face and the fact he could see no sign of even the passage of the smallest creature a cheerful chuckle. Standing up he moved away from the cave-in before patting the dust from his leathers, plucking the light from the wall and starting through the passageways.

Jahaln was sure night had passed it was nigh the end and morning twilight surely rising when he entered the Liche's throne room. There were treasures literally heaped on the floor all about the room. Jahaln had no way of knowing that time had stopped in the world around them and barely noticed the tingling sensation as he watched the dust around the bones on the throne rise up to take form.

"The fates turn." Came the raspy voice, "Join me and share fully of my riches little one, there is much you could gain in my service. I am Jaharadan, ancient high sorcerer to the Dark Council, before they abandoned me to my own means these eons past."

The silent scream of a goddess can turn the unseen events of time.

*   *   *   *   *

Eric felt the ripple in existence and knew time had been suspended, even where he sat working at his computer. Eric looked up, but he was caught in the moment, time stood still. The scream Father!!! echoed in his head. He felt more than heard his daughter's heart wrenching scream and found himself at her side on Ethar without the use of a portal. As it always seemed to happen Eric knew what was going on before he even looked. He even recognized the elevated priest of darkness frozen in time with his dagger held high, the taint of the blade having snared many souls in its twisted history. Eric also knew the shadow flames protecting the young woman's form were his daughter Chareece.

Others also came to her scream, most were kin, he could feel it, but the last to arrive was Merlin Starnook and it seemed understood that all had arrived that were coming. Chareece took form again as ShadowDancer wrapped in the cloak of shadow and flames.

It was Darval, somehow Eric knew who he was, who first spoke, "A time of choosing and a time of judgment has come and this young princess has managed what no ancient before her has done. She has summoned me from another realm!" His hollow laugh echoed emptiness without regret. Morracon dropped to a knee with respect to the Ancients.

Hans Spardic stood by confirming what he already knew inside, he too was an ancient. He wondered though why he was part of this elite gathering.

Eric looked at all who had been summoned and knew that each of them represented a part of her. Tears were in Chareece's eyes. All she said was "Why?" Chareece appeared out of the shadows, but none of the outside gathering could see because she had captured the moment. Some would call it stopping time.

"You have done well to have won the love of these people that they would give their lives for you." Eric smiled knowingly at his daughter. "Her life is forfeit; you must now decide. If you take her soul you can chose to give her back a life, if not it will be taken by this priest of darkness. She has already given it, and it is too late for it not to be taken. You must now decide how you will take care of your people. Everything you do will begin the forming of the rules your followers will know you by."

"Could not have said it better." Gaharias nodded. He noted that perhaps his lineage had more wisdom than he gave credit.

Merlin stepped up to her, "If you bring her back to life, they will start expecting you to do things like that all the time and curse you when you don't. She would feel honored if you held her soul in your bosom to serve you as you willed and you could after this choose your own priests or priestesses, to teach your people this is not what you want."

"So, you are saying I should take her life before the blade hits and keep it never to take another breath, or else my followers might turn against me later." Chareece said with a heavy heart.

Darval chuckled again, "It is all part of the game, the life of a mortal here or there. You have the beginnings of a great following here. Taste of her soul, you may find pleasure in it, reward her friends and family, that is what she wants. Be an ancient that does what her people wish, ah, the word goddess seems to be on the surface of your mind." Chareece shuddered a little understanding what he said.

Hans stepping forward, "If you do not take her soul that dagger will bind her and her kin to a curse. That priest is not really yours. He is none of ours. He is a harbinger of coming wars."

Gaharias looked at Hans. "You my friend are an 'Ancient of War', how long have you known this?"

"Three of us came to Ethar. Two were known by all as Ancients of the new order. Was it not already suspect that three is the number of completing the new beginning? I was changed going through the barrier, which is not the common power. I have been answering requests or pleadings to the Ancients since the war in the Uklian. It is a small matter." Hans stepped back. Looking at Darval he added the comment. "Goddess would be the influence of the human descendants of earth."

Tears ran down her face. "How do I take her soul?"

"You already know, Chareece." Eric placed a hand on her shoulder for comfort. She knew he was right. If she had to do this thing, she did not want to drag it out. She took on the form of ShadowDancer reached out with her heart and the spirit stood up out of the young woman's form and joined them in the captured moment.

Chareece knew her name, Melina. "Sweet Melina, I am honored by your love and claim you to my service. I will honor you offering and care for your family, but I must let my people know I do not wish my followers to die for me." Chareece placed a hand on the shoulder of the young woman's spirit stopping her from kneeling. "Rest now until I call upon you." Melina's spirit wisped and entered into Chareece. Her eyes opened slightly as she sensed the power she gained from the sacrificed soul. She was embarrassed that it felt so good, tasted so sweet as Darval had said it. A temptation she found bothered her that she even felt tempted.

"You did well, Chareece." Eric nodded. "Now let us step back and I will veil our presence and let this play out." They all stepped back and a shimmer surrounded them. Chareece let go of the moment.

The dagger plunged and her blood spilled over the altar. A shocked look crossed the face of the priest as he felt no soul drawn by his dagger knowing the price of failure. A soul had to be taken to serve the purpose of his master as the dagger turned and plunged into his chest. The ground thundered and they felt the darkness rend the continent.

"It is time for ShadowDancer to make an appearance." Chareece shadowed and appeared floating over the altar naked, clothed only in the shadow flames the way her followers knew her, her hair a flowing mix of fire and shadow. "Terriala, come forward."

Another young woman stepped forward, obviously the sister of Melina, "Forgive me ShadowDancer." She knelt before the altar, "I was not pure as my sister or I would have given myself as the firstborn." Tears of regret and shame were in her eyes.

"I will keep your sister always close to me, but I want my followers to live for me, not die. I am making you my high priestess to see that no other shed their blood on an altar for me. You will see your sister again for she shall be my messenger to you. I charge you with seeing to it that my followers live and lead people in the caring for those who are in need. I will send you further instructions, but first rise and face our followers."

Terriala stood up and turned to face the rest of the gathering. ShadowDancer gestured and Terriala's garments were transformed into a scant outfit Black silk with golden trim with a coat of arms that looked like Eric's hanging between her breasts only with a wisp of flame over the back of the lion. In the right hand of Terriala appeared a Scepter with a flame at the top of mixed fire and shadow that continues to burn. ShadowDancer spoke with a voice that tugged at every ear. "Know my priestess." ShadowDancer Vanished into the shadows and Chareece appeared again in the company of the Ancients.

"Again, you did well daughter." Eric stated, and then turned to the rest of the company. "Destiny has called this company together; I believe we have matters to discuss. I am sure we all felt the evil that awoke." Chareece looked at her father, she wanted to know the land he came from, why he was so different from the rest.

"Let's head to my place then." Gaharias stated, "A little safer to speak there then here."

Darval shook his head. "I have been undetected for hundreds of years, I am sure my place is more secure." They all agreed, and he took the group with him.

*   *   *   *   *

Arco was eying a small thicket on the side of the road. He was looking for a place to camp down for the night. It was not safe to travel at night for even a large party and now there were only the two of them. Vorka, his wife was also eying the setting sun and knew the dangers of being in the open after dark. Her specialty was plants, but she wasn't ignorant to common knowledge. She was well known in her dwarf homeland for her battle skills also. Right now they had to concern themselves with disappearing.

This morning before sunrise there had still been twelve of them. Arco and Vorka had gone to get more wood for their breakfast fire when another one of those hideous black clouds with that suffocating sulfur smell suddenly blew down on them. If they had not been used to the darkness of their caves back in the mountains, they might have lost each other.

The deep grumbling from the belly of Ethar began, joined by the sounds of fleeing animals crashing blindly through the forest. All they could do was to wait it out; the ground of Ethar was shaking too violently to stand, so they just clung to each other to keep from being separated and for comfort. Suddenly there was an eerie silence that sat for a few moments. Then as suddenly as it was silent the ground heaved with a sudden wrench and a sound as of a thousand claps of thunder at once in every direction. It hurled them into an uncontrolled roll across the ground. Then it stopped.

Everything was still. It felt like a long time before a breeze started lifting the darkness and the air finally cleared, but left a dust covering on everything. When his head cleared Arco realized how tightly he was holding Vorka. He loosened his embrace a little and that brought Vorka back also. They stood up together, looked around and back into the others face. They had both been in quakes before, but this one was close and large, too close and too large.

They started searching for their camp or where it should have been. They made a hard stop and took a step back at what they found, the ground gaped open as though gouged open by a mighty sword. The open ravine ran north and south as far as the eye could see and the bottom was filled with the molten blood of Ethar. They could not see clear enough at the distance across the ravine, especially with the heat distortion to know if there was anything of their camp on the other side. There was no doubt in their minds what was left of the rest of their small party. All they had was what they were wearing.

They both had swords and knives. He had his bow, and she had her sling. They were wearing leather armor and had what they needed to survive. It took longer to inventory their bruises and aches then their belongings, but neither had any serious injuries or broken bones. If either had a concussion, it was minor and no outward indications.

There was not much to consider concerning the choice to go back or continue. The gap in the ground blocked their way back which made for a quick easy decision. It was thirteen days travel on foot to the next city, unless they pushed it, then they might be able to make it in seven days. The first day was half gone before they could even get started.

They set into motion without delay; survival did not allow time to mourn. Arco and Vorka also decided in a quick conversation that for now they did not want to think about the fate of their friends. If the others had survived, they were separated by the rip that tore through the land. If the grace that saved them spared their friends and companions, they were forced to travel in different directions now. They would hunt and scavenge in route; spring had a bounty of nourishment everywhere. While the quake had stripped most of the bounty to spoils on the ground they had sufficient fortune to take care of their needs. This day would be the safest for travel after the turmoil. It was best to get as far as possible for the following day would bring deaths lurkers. Wolves, scavengers, and death lurkers would be on the prowl, they always are after a disaster.

Looking to their arrival at Efra they knew they would need something to exchange for supplies to continue the rest of the way to The Walled City of Talmorg. They would hunt for pelts, herbs and medicines in route. This first day however they would just travel eating only berries and fruit that gave up their bounty easily in route and there were plenty. They had thanked the Ancients many times for no further incidents as they hurried along that day and there were none. They had walked a healthy pace without stopping and traveled more then they normally would in a full day.

"Vorka, let's check 'en nare," Arco said after looking over a thicket with shrubbery around its perimeter. They walked back off the road. The clearing was about ten paces from the road and about seven across.

"Ground here is clear en good."   Vorka said after poking around and checking the bushes. Her knowledge of the plants and land had always been useful in a very practical way. They also had a great deal of knowledge that Arco had learned as a Bard. He memorized every song, ballad, legend and story he had ever heard. That is part of what lead him to being a swordsman in the beginning.

Arco wanted to be sure and thrust his sword down, good solid ground. "Very well." He fumbled around in his pockets "Ah, there it is." He pulled out a small bundle of pipes, examined them carefully, and then began piping an eerie tune casting an enchantment of protection around their chosen camp. Nothing could have protected them from the morning disaster. He yanked his mind back from the dark thoughts; he could not afford to let his anguish surface, not at least until Vorka was in a safe place.

They set camp without a fire. Deciding that the risk of the fire bringing crazed people this night was greater than the risk of animals or anything a fire might protect them from. They set their tent to a low profile, more of a makeshift lean-to, set so that it could not be seen from the road in the low shrubbery. They huddled close using their cloaks for cover, finding solace in the warmth of each other's embrace. Neither really slept well. Vorka woke up screaming twice in the night, Arco kissed and snuggled her until she calmed down again each time.

Morning came. They ate a quiet meal of hard bread sweetened with a berry paste and water. They cleaned up their camp and packed their gear and headed down the road. They continued to come across a large number of animals killed by the quake that were still fresh enough to salvage hides and parts. Arco sang a song of warding as they walked, protecting them from passing eyes. Many animals did pass still showing fear and edginess, but as a few more days passed, everything seemed to calm. The further they got and the more time that passed the less corpses they found along the way. Arco figured there were two reasons, first the further they got from the source the less impact and second, the more time that passed the more the scavengers of the woods would clean things up.

While dwarfs did not have the knowledge and instincts of an elf above ground, they were not without their share of adventure and experience. It seemed the safer things seemed, the more the weight of their lost friends crept into the corners of their minds. Vorka and Arco were much quieter than they normally were but pressed on with purpose.

CHAPTER 2

Gathering Forces

Lord Valdir awoke from his slumber, pushed back his cover and stared at the ceiling. How much time had passed? He had stopped counting so many years ago. The day was getting close, he could feel it, when they would cross the oceans again and lay claim to long forgotten lands. He had been promised with a vision of the future, having been locked in a trance with the Ancient Darval. That had been a long time ago, but every time he slept, he saw it again in his dreams. It was a short vision, but he was standing there on the rocky precipice watching his armies as they poured inland by the thousands, to reclaim the land of the middle continents that had once been theirs.

He had ruled his people in this land of chaos ever since the fall. This was a harsh place and no living souls had dare tread here intentionally since long before the fall. Darval had said then that this was its redeeming quality; even the Ancients of their enemies would only search it during the daylight. Not finding any living souls, they would depart not seeing the threat. The place and its occupants were alike in many ways. Neither lived, yet neither knew the comforts and rest of deaths sweet waiting.

Lord Valdir roared as he flew up and over the edge of his casket. "I shall again taste of the blood of life." he said as he landed on his feet, "so long denied me!"

There was a widespread creaking and sliding sound of hinges and stone on stone, followed by the rustling of cloth. "Rise up my slothful Legions the time is near at hand and we have preparations to make. It is time to commit our every resource to prepare for crossing the seas. By the Ancients I sure could use a blood wine!" A golden goblet, dressed in gems fit only for those who came before appeared on the table by his sarcophagus, a sure sign from the Ancients that it was time.

"My Lord finally wearies of waiting." Came the sneering whisper of Balgrin, closing out with a hissed snarl.

"Nay, my power-lusting grunge heap, as you can plainly see if you look the Ancients are telling me themselves, our time to return to walk against the world of the living has come." He held forth the goblet for all to see and drank of the cup, laughing when it did not empty, yet filled his veins with strength he had not felt in millennium. "Come to me and drink to our victory over exile."

Had it been so long, he had forgotten why he lusted for the taste of fresh blood, the one thing that overthrew his ability to maintain reason. With the first taste from the goblet that lust had returned stronger than it had ever been before. He looked at the goblet again; there was something wrong with it he could not place. It was not the goblet of the Ancients at all. A shudder passed through him as he felt himself being bent to the will of another. A dead laugh echoed in the back of his mind. Balgrin also drank from the cup before he realized and before he could give warning. Soon his will would be so bent he would not want to give warning anyway. The moments of regret passed.

"Summon all of our legions, we have wars to fight."

*   *   *   *   *

Jahaln followed his new master Jaharadan. The ground shook when he struck the bargain with the lich Jaharadan, but it was a promise of abundance for him and the only way he saw clear to get out of this maze of the deceased. Jahaln noticed that Jaharadan had a sudden burst of strength and appeared to shift closer to the likeness of the living as the ground shook and mumbled something about a stupid priest. "So, if the Dark Council abandoned you, how is it you still live? I mean this place is not exactly abounding with sustenance of any kind."

"In studying the magic of the dead, I learned much of the magic of extended life. You are fortunate Jahaln your timing is right that I need a new high servant to lead my minions. I need another now to replace my high priest who foolishly let the soul of a young virgin slip from his grasp and gave up his own soul to feed me instead." He laughed a dark laugh. "I learned some of the powers of the Ancients while in their service. I shall return now as one of them. You know we can all achieve that greatness if we learn enough and gain enough power."

Jahaln raised an eyebrow, "So you are saying even I could become an ancient?"

"Sure, my young apprentice and I shall teach you. First we must get back up to the forests where my followers await and submit their petitions to be granted rights as High priest." Jaharadan made a gesture and the ground that formed a wall bound together with roots in front of them parted exposing an ancient spiral stairway leading up. Jahaln knew he would never have found that on his own.

The stairs led to another door that opened into a stone room overrun with cobwebs, carved stone, and stone coffins. Jahaln noticed no other footprints in the dust as they stepped out through the sepulcher into the cool night air of the cemetery. The cemetery was overrun by the forest and underbrush. Jaharadan moved quickly expecting Jahaln to keep up. "Before we get there, be careful, I have granted you power from my own." He pointed to their left.

"This way quickly, they are gathered and waiting. You must look upon them as if they are insignificant to you. Pull up your cowl and cloak."

There was a gathering of about forty seemingly a random selection from all races. Jaharadan raged up to the altar. Jahaln stayed at his right side as if an attachment to his robes. "So, my High Priest has failed me and not one of you thought to accomplish his service in his short-coming." The crowd cowered to their knees.

"If I had soulcatcher I would get your willing sacrifice of a virgin. I would not fail." A voice came from a woman in the mix.

"Step forwards would be priestess. What makes you so sure you would succeed where your predecessor failed." The dagger hovered in the air above the altar where he summoned it.

She came forwards and knelt before Jaharadan. "I will succeed in three days or I will serve you as the willing sacrifice."

Jaharadan bent over and took her chin in his bony fingers. The young woman aged visibly and then was restored. "Your offer is accepted. With your success will grant you the position of High Priestess. Your failure you have committed to my service. Either way you earn your place in my service. Now go quickly and use your time wisely, Aranise. The rest of you will return in three days with twenty followers each by whatever means you can. It is time to start building my army. Your minions will answer to Jahaln when the time comes." Jaharadan lead Jahaln back into the forest.

"You seem to have a plan; I am sure it is good with the time you have had to make it. Tell me what it is that I can do to uphold my end of our bargain." Jahaln followed Jaharadan his mentor and leader and his ticket to a better life.

"I have minions moving getting ready to move from the forbidden continents. They do not yet know that they serve me. I have much to teach you before I can put you in command of them. This will hurt a little, but it is the quickest way to give you basic knowledge I need you to have." Jaharadan placed his hands on Jahaln's head, and everything went black.

*　　*　　*　　*　　*

Aranise got up as commanded and departed straight away. She headed straight to the Wonk village she knew that was not too far away. It used to be her home. She knew a small farm on the outskirts. "They have a daughter." She whispered to herself as she ran through the forest. She reached the outskirts of the farm and watched carefully, uttering incantations under her breath as she explored the farm. Finally, she had the whole family in the house, and she walked to the front door. She walked in and the daughter she had already selected was the only one to look at her or see her.

"What was your name young one?"

"Karrine." The young girl answered uncertainty in her eyes.

Aranise looked at the father. "Cut your hand with your fork." She instructed and the man picked the fork up like a zombie and scraped the tongs across his palm causing it to bleed. "Now Karrine, you see I have control over your family. It is up to you what will happen now."

Fear now filled Karrine's face. Aranise had her where she wanted her. The young girl would willingly give herself to save her family.

*　　*　　*　　*　　*

Jahaln opened his eyes and saw the ceiling of the crypt. He wondered how long he had been here, wherever here was. Rolling over he realized he was in a stone coffin. Amazingly comfortable he thought, with a shiver. He sat up and looked around. The swelling of knowledge that Jaharadan planted in his mind suddenly started rushing through his thoughts. He explored the knowledge and found that it was his. While it was still chaotic, it had become a part of his very being. Along with the knowledge of manipulating powers like Jaharadan, he realized he had learned bits and pieces of the creature's life. To test the practicality of all that he now seemed to know, he started experimenting. He found he could levitate things around the room, he could cast lightening and had control over how powerful it was.

Jahaln sat up and climbed out of the coffin with relative ease. He felt Jaharadan outside and went out to join him. "Good my apprentice you are up. You will not miss the sacrifice then. Let us return to the thicket." Jaharadan carried a large jewel encrusted golden bowl and placed it at the bottom of the altar in a place that looked designed for this purpose. "Here she comes."

As Jaharadan spoke, Aranise stepped into the open with the young girl silently following. The young girl did as Aranise had instructed her, preparing herself according to ritual dropping her robe before the altar and lying down on the cold stone. She kept her mind on her family, closing her eyes so that she could not see what was commencing around her.

"Do you give yourself willingly?" The ladies voice asked

"I give myself willingly." It felt like a dream. Then something cold seemed to be drawing her out of her chest. This was not what she had expected. In her mind she screamed out for help, hoping the Ancients would hear her. The freezing ache encompassed her.

Jahaln watched the blood drain into the bowl and watched Aranise pour it into a ritual goblet. "Now, both of you drink with me." Jaharadan said taking the first drink of the goblet, then holding it up to Jahaln and Aranise in turn. Jahaln felt the power surging through him and sensing the increase in power of both his counter parts in the circle. Jaharadan's appearance changed dramatically, taking on the appearance of life, no longer the decayed look of the dead. His flesh filled in and he did not even look particularly old.

Aranise smiled wickedly at Jahaln, and then looking back at Jaharadan, "I bind my soul to you, my lord." Taking the sacrificial dagger, she sliced her hand open and let a portion of blood drain into the goblet before wrapping her hand. She offered the goblet again to Jaharadan with a look of victory in her eyes as she glanced at Jahaln.

Jaharadan drank and handed the goblet to Jahaln and said "Drink, my apprentice." Aranise was visibly shaken when Jahaln drank from the goblet. She dropped to her knees and bowed her head to each of them in turn.

Jahaln gave her a cool detached look stating as he turned with Jaharadan to walk away, "We will see you at the gathering tomorrow, Priestess Aranise."

*　　*　　*　　*　　*

Milmorgs were shy and friendly by nature. It surprised Jahaln how easily he could turn a cold shoulder to Aranise. He also noticed as life was restored to Jaharadan his mentor grew more in appearance to something between a gnome and a Milmorg. This would suggest that Jaharadan was thousands of years old. From the thoughts and memories infused into his mind, he knew Jaharadan had found ways of exploring the world through the realm of the dead while sustained by the souls of others he stole when they got to close. He also saw how Jaharadan gathered the souls his priests and priestesses gathered with sacrifices using daggers like soul-catchers.

"Draw the power from the life around you Jahaln, we have no time for daydreaming, you must practice if you are going to master and retain what you now know."

"Yes, Master." Jahaln focused again and drew in the power as one takes in a breath. He could feel the bugs in the ground around him shrivel and die; there was an expanding ring of dead plants around him. He raised his hand pointing into the ground at the buried coffin he could not see with his eyes. The ground above burst open, and the skeletal creature climbed out. This time at least it appeared to have all its parts in the right places. He instructed it to go stand with the rest of the beginnings of his ragtag army of minions.

The glint of a ring on the skeleton's finger caught his attention. Under his bidding, the skeleton removed the ring and threw it to him. It was a royal signet ring of elfish origin. Jahaln wondered how an elf royal cemetery wound up over run and abandoned. "So, this is a royal burial ground?"

"Indeed, But Darval and his followers Vanished into the Shadows long ago. Else we would not so easily have summoned his armies and the armies of the dark council to our command. At least we can control those that remain?" Jaharadan stepped back. "If we are going to be a success, you will need to summon them more than one at a time. Go for twenty this time."

Jahaln held his hands out to both sides, palms up, drawing in the power, then suddenly releasing. The graves around him burst open, and exactly twenty more rose up out of the ground. As he instructed them, they formed up with the rest of the dead army.

"I suspected you would do well." Jaharadan laughed. "You have an army that needs nothing from you and has no fear. You need however other minions that cannot be so easily dispelled. We have a start though."

*　　　*　　　*　　　*　　　*

Lord Valdir sat calmly on his stone pedestal watching as the minions of old Deamorg filed in and through everyone had to drink of the cup. This new ancient demanded every last one bound to direct loyalty. Balgrin perched near also watching with the same blank stare. His deeper thoughts were not far from those of Lord Valdir. Thousands had passed through already and the line still looked endless. The Minions of Deamorg were no small force. This new ancient did not have respect for domestic members of the clans. Even the children were being pulled in as part of this disposable army.

Lord Valdir sat calmly on his stone pedestal watching as the minions of old Deamorg filed in and through everyone had to drink of the cup. This new ancient demanded every last one bound to direct loyalty. Balgrin perched near also watching with the same blank stare. His deeper thoughts were not far from those of Lord Valdir. Thousands had passed through already and the line still looked endless. The Minions of Deamorg were no small force. This new ancient did not have respect for domestic members of the clans. Even the children were being pulled in as part of this disposable army.

Their free will was taken, and their service was bound, but below the surface brewed a growing hatred for this master to which they found themselves bound. Deeper thoughts sought for a way to rebel against the bonds. Their minds called out to Darval in hope that he might deliver them from their subjugation

*   *   *   *   *

Keldin had been a quiet Milmorg Village. Even the Scaldorian wars, while a lot of residence had been drafted into the army it did not impact the village too much. The new religious organization that seemed to spring up overnight was already causing more disturbances. Captain Racken the local Peace Officer had five disappearances to investigate since the group sprang up. The members of the group were very closed mouthed about the inner workings unless you joined. They were very open about promoting the worship of Jaharadan "The Ancient of the Milmorgs". In the past, before the council of the Ancients and the split, Darval had been their ancient and took good care of them. Some say he still did.

Racken knew personally that Gaharias had taken care of him and his family in the absence of Darval. He also knew that others of the Ancients had a hand in taking care of their people. From what he could find on Jaharadan there was never an ancient by this name. The closest on record was a powerful sorcerer that worked for Darval before the Wars of the Ancients. He had disappeared around the time of the disappearance of the Dark Council and was presumed to have gone with them or died. Racken weighed the possibility that the Dark Council had made him a member, but then why the openness of the order and secrecy of what they do. It would have made sense if it were the other way around. This order also demanded dedicated loyalty to Jaharadan which was so contrary to the ways of any other Ancients.

The disappearances all seemed somehow associated, but not traceable back to the order. Rumors were that the order was doing live sacrifices, but rumors are usually worse than reality and tended to grow. The sources of those rumors seemed to always get converted and the story always changed. There were no laws governing weapons and armor, but it did bother Racken that the order of Jaharadan seemed to be arming up for war. Racken had reported events in Keldin back to the Milmorg High Council and learned that it was happening all over the United City States of Rackenwolf. The military felt the internal threat, but it would be too hard on the civilian populace to over recruit. Then there were members of the military that had joined the order, so communication on the subject was done with extreme caution.

The sect of Jaharadanians seemed to hold followers. None of those who had joined the sect would leave. When anyone attempted to pull them away, they would start chanting all the great things that Jaharadan has done for them. Racken noted that some of the feats attributed to Jaharadan by his followers were done by others and some of them seemed made up with no historical support. Racken would not go to any of their gatherings either. It seemed that anyone who went to a gathering was converted no matter how opposed they were before going. He did not trust what went on.

Racken made sure he was securely hidden as he watched the group of the new order moving up the alley from house to house, knocking on doors and offering something to drink. People he would not have expected were joining the group. Nobody seemed to be casting; he figured it must be the drink. Those who were not members of this new order were soon to be the exception and Racken was confident it would not be safe for anyone who did not join. It was then he made his decision; he must travel to the seat of Gaharias in hopes of saving at least a remnant of his people.

Racken slipped out of town. As he scribed the note and attached it to the bird's leg, he hoped that the chief or the guards was not lost to the persuasion of the new cult yet. He released the bird, and it took off through the air. Racken made a familiar clicking sound and his lizard mount was by his side. Adjusting the saddle, he climbed on. The lizards of the Rackenwolf were much faster than any horse and a much better fit to the size of a Milmorg. The saddle fit just behind the front legs and the movement of the ride was much smoother then that of a horse. The only up and down movement was with the contour of the ground, there was instead some swaying and twisting movement instead. Racken had never left his homeland from which his name was derived. He and his lizard headed to the east and a couple verses from the never-ending poem came to mind.

Through the Rackenwolf he'll ride,
The Milmorg homes pass in stride,
He'll travel through the mother's ridge,
And come upon a crack to bridge,

A hope for friends that he might reach,
If he can cross the burning breach,
He'll find a way to cross the gap,
To save the land from the liche's trap.

*   *   *   *   *

Lord Rolland was leading the evacuation. They were abandoning the Barony of Pendril. Nothing had actually happened yet, but they chose to head the warnings of the seers. First the seers had the visions of the dead rising and taking over the Barony. It was built on an ancient battlefield which was part of the heritage of the castle. "The dead are returning. We must leave before they get here." Then more people started having the dreams. There was debate, but in the end, they chose to heed the warnings. Every cart and wagon were used and every provision that could be secured for travel. They were not sure where they were going at first, but they headed west. It was the eighth day of travel when they saw Shadow Keep in the distance. That would be a good place to rest while they decided what to do next.

Relief passed back through the caravan when the word of stopping at Shadow Keep was passed back. Spirits were picking up. Lord Rolland ordered an emissary party to ride ahead and announce their intent. As the small group started to take lead ahead of them, the ground lurched followed by a booming thundering sound. Nothing was left standing in the caravan, people, horses, wagons were all thrown to the ground. The series of tremors that followed were minor, but it was even longer before anyone recovered enough to start getting back to their feet.

Lord Rolland called back the emissary team. He wanted to assess their situation now before sending messengers ahead. There would be injured, and their supplies would have to be picked up and wagons repaired. Shadow Keep was still a day's ride away. It took hours to regroup and set camp. The repairs needed on the wagons exceeded the materials they had to accomplish the task. He knew that Shadow Keep had to have suffered also and wondered just how much help they would be able to provide. "Captain Serreck take a few men and help organize the tradesman so that we can get our people provided for."

"Yes, my Lord." Captain Serreck answered and called out to a few other officers and disappeared back into the crowd.

Captain Aramson stepped up. "Lord, we have everything scribed and I think we are ready to head to Shadow Keep again."

"Very Good. It is late and you can wait until morning to start." Lord Rolland nodded. "Perhaps we will have some better information by then also."

"As you wish Lord Rolland." Captain Aramson gave a respectful nod. "We shall help set up the encampment then."

Faylynn tugged at Rolland's arm, "Come and eat. You cannot lead your people if you do not keep up your strength, my husband."

He turned, "Thank you, my dear." Putting his arm around her shoulder he followed her lead to a place near the fire to sit and eat.

*   *   *   *   *

Gaharias continued, "There are changes happening all over Ethar and as much as I would like to hope that the quake that ripped through the whole world was because of Chareece, we all know that it was the awakening of something much darker."

"I know I have responded to requests made from all the major continents and the minor ones with one exception, the dead continent. There does seem to be an increase of trouble everywhere." Eric stated his agreement. The others added their words and nods of agreement or acknowledgment.

"The Ancients of the council can not intervene directly in the affairs of races, we can answer requests, and we can grant boons and select champions among our people. That means my hands are tied and the hands of the council in ways that the rest of you are not bound. We are not helpless, but the rest of you here can do more to directly assist the peoples of Ethar." Gaharias looked at the rest of those present.

Hans laughed, "The rest of us here are not bound by that oath. Darval and the dark council never signed the accord. Merlin is a power to be reckoned with, but not an "ancient". Chareece is second generation new ancient or goddess. Eric and I are of the new order of Ancients our part in things is not yet carved out."

Darval leaned his elbow on the stone table. "I have my races and my people here in the Shadow Realms. We have created a world here and none of us intends on returning. There are remnants of peoples that we owe the choice of coming to join us or remaining on Ethar. As you know this place is out of the normal reach of the Council of Ancients and the older ones on Ethar. I welcome you to use my place to meet and plan as you need it."

"You have no vested interest in the fate of Ethar?" Chareece asked a bit surprised.

"I have some of my people to gather from the dead continent and I will always give those who were my followers the option to come to the Shadow Realms. Beyond that you are right niece." Darval leaned back in his chair.

"There is nothing else for us to do here right now." Merlin piped up, "We each need to gather information as we can and keep the lines of communication open. Until we know more of what we face, we cannot make any plans."

Darval slid a coin to Merlin, "I don't know what your part is in this matter, but you are the only one that cannot return and leave from here by your own means. This coin will give you passage." Merlin scooped up the coin and it vanished.

"Hans," Eric caught his attention, "before we depart, I have something I want to give you." Standing up he moved where he could talk with Hans in more private conversation.

Hans followed, "What is it Eric?"
"Bonny and I will be getting married on Earth. We wanted you to be there, but you need to clear up matters of the police thinking you are dead or worse if you are going to be able to come." Pulling the dragon amulet out he handed it to Hans, "This will give you the ability to travel back and forth from earth at will. It is much like mine. This way you can go back and forth as you wish instead of having to come to me."

Hans looked at it with uncertainty, "Thank you, I think." It had been years since he had left earth and he had no urge to go back. He would make an exception for Eric and Bonny, to attend their wedding he would go back. They had been friends for a long time. The others started leaving. "I assume the things you told me about the time shifting with yours will work for this also?"

The others finished departing. Eric looked over and back to Hans. "I have not tested it, but it should. You'll want to practice with it some to be sure of what you can and can't do." Eric looked to be sure the rest were gone. "It has other attributes too, I have not completely mastered the art of making items, they always seem to do more then I intended. That is just a warning to be careful."

"Perhaps now is as good a time as any to start experimenting." He dropped the gold chain around his neck and let the dragon hang for a moment. He thought about his house in the small college town and a moment later he was standing in the living room. He had not actually been ready to go, but now he knew how sensitive the amulet could be.

Looking around he could tell that someone had searched the house, although they did not make a mess. All draws and doors were slightly ajar, and things were all moved and out of place. He looked around for something to tell him what day and what time it was. Leaving the living room, he went to his office and powered up the computer. Eric had kept his rent and bills caught up; they had agreed to that when he decided to stay on Ethar. He shut drawers and doors while the computer booted up. Six months had passed. He had been on Ethar for years, decades even. He had gotten married, and his son was already twenty-five years old. This confirmed that time was not a constant between dimensions. He was confident that he would return to Ethar within moments of when he left, no matter how long he spent clearing things up here.

He was Jaffro Jamis here, he had to remember that. For him, it had been almost 30 years since he had been called by that name. His armor was inappropriate here. Slipping to his bedroom, Jaffro stuffed his armor into a pillowcase and put on something more appropriate from the draws. He made his way back to the front door.

He was Jaffro Jamis here, he had to remember that. For him, it had been almost 30 years since he had been called by that name. His armor was inappropriate here. Slipping to his bedroom, Jaffro stuffed his armor into a pillowcase and put on something more appropriate from the draws. He made his way back to the front door.

Opening the door, he pulled down the Police tape that barred the opening. There was another plastic barricade of tape around the perimeter of the property. The lawn was unkempt, but then nobody would have been crossing the police line to mow it. Jaffro was uncertain what exactly to do. There were no police monitoring the place, so he just proceeded to clean the place up. He would take things as they came.

It was the next day officer Terrell stopped by with lots of questions. The officer seemed surprised, but glad to see him. Jaffro answered questions without lies, yet not telling too much, sidestepping some things. After a while officer Terrell decided he had enough information and was not going to get anything more. There was no crime and no real reason to try and force additional information out of anyone. There really is no law against someone taking off on what might be called a walk-about. He explained he had just left the area and spent time with some friends he made, and then Jaffro started asking if there was a crime or something in the area that required the police knowing details of his whereabouts or some other reason, he should be obligated to share everything he has been doing. Officer Terrell did not feel he had any legitimate reason to probe or impose any further in Jaffro's life. He apologized explaining the extended absence had aroused suspicions of possible foul-play and they had been obligated to investigate his disappearance.

Before heading back to Ethar he sat for a while in his big easy chair in the living room. There are advantages to having a place to go to get away and clear his head and still get back to ShadowKeep without losing time. Jaffro also noted that while he had been on Ethar for about 30 years he had not apparently aged and was in much better physical condition then when he left. He realized too that none of them, Bonny, Eric, nor himself had any indication of aging on Ethar during this large expanse of time either. He took the amulet in his hand again.

*   *   *   *   *

Darvarias had stood up from the mat where he had just completed another session of magic training with his mom when the sound thundered from the ground and the world turned upside down in a flash. He saw the house collapsing and with a blink of the eyes he and his mom were outside in the front yard being tossed around by the quake. When the ground stopped they were both alright aside from minor bruises, but the house was a pile of debris. They looked around and the entire village was leveled. They did not hesitate to think about it, but immediately jumped to their feet and without a word rushed to the neighbor's house.

The two children had been playing in the yard, while they were a little beat up they were basically okay also. "Yell if you can hear us." Darvarias shouted at the fallen home. Both Darvarias and Stralina used their magic to search the debris and clear a path to the children's mom to get her out.

"She is here." Stralina yelled, "She is hurt." With a gesture a curtain snapped form a window on a fallen wall and slipped under the lady lifting her and carrying her clear of the house.

Darvarias put out a small fire in what was the kitchen area of the house. "There is no one else here." There were others moving around the ruins of the village helping their neighbors. Darvarias moved to the next home, his mom could take care of the woman she was fussing over in the yard.

As he approached the remains of the house, he heard a man yelling, "Help, My wife and kids are under there. Someone please help!"

He found the man trapped by his legs under a wall. "Where are they, neighbor? Calm down and just point." The man pointed. Darvarias focused, he could sense the woman and one of the kids.

"Help them." Desperation touched the man's voice.

Darvarias blew across his hand towards the area the debris started lifting and piling off to the side of the foundation. Once it was cleared to the floor, he levitated the three bodies and moved them over to the front yard. "Stay still." He barked. Gestured and the wall lifted off the man's legs. Darvarias levitated the man over with his family and knelt down to check them all out.

He did everything he knew to keep them alive. The mother and the young boy Darvarias knew would survive, the youngest a girl was not breathing, and he brought her back three times. He didn't have any official healing training. He looked over where Stralina was tending to the woman. The woman was sitting up and taking a drink. "Mom!"

Stralina looked up and then jumped up and ran over to where he was, "What is the situation?"

"The girl needs you. I have done what I could but keep losing her. The others are stable if you can take care of her, I'll move on to the next house." He looked at her with confidence in her skills.

Looking at the girl not even looking up she said. "Go."

Soldiers started arriving to help and set up a base camp and medical center. Shadow Keep, not too far away, did not look like it had fared to well either. There were dead and injured and the destruction was massive. It would be the same in every town and village hit by the quake. Those who could work worked late into the night. Disaster brought them all together and they all worked for the common good.

*　　*　　*　　*　　*

Eric stepped out of their bedroom. Bonny looked up and saw the concern on his face and knew it had to be something stirring on Ether. She already knew something was up. As an ancient she got her share of requests and pleads to the Ancients for help. There had been a dramatic increase in the short time that Eric was gone. She had learned how to capture the moment, stop time as far as she could tell, so that she could deal with those requests without losing the flow of whatever she was doing. Even with that, she got so distracted that her mom kept asking her if she was alright.

"What is it Eric?"

"Events of some kind are starting, they may need us there, I don't know." Eric was making no effort to hide their conversation from her mom. They had told her everything already and she played it off as a game they play.

"You must have more than that." Bonny looked at his distracted expression. A plea came to her ear and she suspended the moment almost by instinct. It was a young girl who called her. She lived in the village by Shadow Keep. Bonny only had a glimpse of the damage. She pulled the girls parents from the burning remains of the house with a thought and spread a healing aura over as much of the area as she could in the moment. It would save the lives of many. What she did she knew overstepped the rules that bound the council, but she was not a part of the council of Ancients. The moment passed.

"Yes, dear, I do, but it is bits and pieces that do not fit together yet." Eric grabbed a glass of water from the kitchen sink while they conversed in whispers, "There are good and bad things happening, but scattered events. Chareece has come into herself as ShadowDancer. I am sure that Talmorg doesn't know yet and her dual identity has not slipped out to any who should not know."

"Ok, that is part of the good." Bonny just left that hanging knowing there had to be more.

"Darval is back and working with us. Well not back but working with us. Whatever, we met outside of the reach of the council." Eric Sipped his water and scratched his jaw in thought.

Bonny shook her head, "I don't think that is the bad stuff you mentioned." She wanted to know what he knew and what it had to do with the request she just answered.

"A deceiver, a follower of some dark force convinced a follower of ShadowDancer to let herself be sacrificed on the alter to her goddess. Chareece had to take her soul before the dagger, a soul stealer took her. Not getting her soul the dagger turned on its wielder." Eric did not hide the concern in his face for Chareece.

"Am I going to have to draw every piece of information out of you?" She asked in a terse tone.

"No," He looked up, "I am sorry, just trying to think things through as I tell you." He shifted setting his water glass down. "Something awakened when that dagger turned. There is a rip from pole to pole on Ethar. There is trouble stirring everywhere and there is a religious cult or many religious cults growing following a very dark order."

"That is what did that damage!" She said revealing she knew something already.

Surprise did not even make a full showing on his face as he quickly realized she would also be getting the requests for intercession by the peoples of Ethar. "Indeed, it was felt around the world. I am sure there will be quakes that are smaller in the aftermath too."

"The village in Shadow Valley was leveled. I hope Hans, Stralina and Darvarias are all ok." Taking a sip from her coffee she had been drinking while talking with her mom, "Did you get the amulet to Hans?"

"Sure did, he is probably at home now, just guessing. I am glad we kept all his bills and everything current."

Bonny nodded, "He still has to clear everything up with the police, but I don't think there is any law against disappearing for a period of time."

"It was almost 6 months and I have no idea how or if he will explain it." Eric chuckled, "He does not legally have to explain his absence, but I am sure he will be asked. The weird part will probably be stepping back in time thirty years and finding things like they were that long ago."

"He'll be fine. It will just take some getting used to." looking back from the window, "He has already mowed and cleaned up the yard from all that police tape and barricades."

Eric paused as he was interrupted by another request from someone on the small island continent south of the middle continents. They were a peaceful land and the people never seemed to ask for much, but their continent had been ripped in half. They had taken a lot of damage, by the quake and by the waves of ocean that flooded over their land afterward. Eric noted that other Ancients were being generous with their responses to calls for help from this land also. These people actually did not belong to any one ancient, they were built from adventurers and others who wandered by sea from their homelands and happened to land here. Their water supply had been contaminated by the waves of ocean, and the spring fed freshwater lake was lost to ocean water that filled the crack dividing their land. Eric turned some of the springs that had fed the lake causing them to form fountains from the hills near the new divide and also caused a gentle rain to begin falling filling containers that were placed outdoors with fresh water.

"Bonny, they need us. We need to attend to whatever we need to here and go to Ethar." Eric looked at the clock. "We can spend as much time there as we need to and still return before the night is through here."

Bonny nodded, "That sounds like a plan, but where shall we stay while we are there? If it is known where we stay, the masses may seek our audience and then we will get little done."

"We can deal with that when we are there."

CHAPTER 3

Picking Up Pieces

Hans stepped back from the portal to what was left of the parapet on outer wall of Shadow Keep. The destruction around him was so utterly complete. Shadow Keep had withstood the onslaught of dozens of attempts throughout history and remained standing and solid. Eric had told him that the crack went from pole to pole, for some reason he had not considered the impact. Concern for his wife and son now nagged at him. He made his way to a command post set up in a cleared area where the outer marketplace was previously.

"Captain, where is the High Lord and the central command center?"

"Lord Spardic," The Captain saluted, "It is good to see you made it. We have had no sign nor word from the High Lord yet. What is left of the internal regiments went to help salvage and support the people in the village. We have 12 command posts around the keep, but none has been established as the central command since you are the first of the High Command to have surfaced, we will follow your lead on that until the High Lord surfaces."

Returning the salute, "There was a caravan riding this way at a day's travel away, have we heard any word from them yet?"

"No, sir, at least no word has reached this camp. They would probably come here first."

"Have we heard any word on the affairs of the village?" Hans looked around, "We'll make this the Central command for now. I want a squad specifically dedicated to finding the High Lord."

"We have initial reports that the village was leveled. Stralina and Darvarias are playing key parts in salvaging what is there and helping survivors." The Captain was watching Hans' expression suspecting that was the news he wanted to hear. "We have no statistical information yet. We are focused on survivors and reorganization for now."

"Set me up a table and chair over here. To effectively coordinate efforts, I'll have to remain in one location so I can be located until the High Lord or some other Higher-ranking lord can take over."

"Very good, My Lord."

"I'll need the current chain of command and twelve messengers, one for each of our camps and one for the Village. If we have the names, I will need the names of who is currently in charge of each camp."

"As you command, My Lord." The other officers and men around him had been setting about accomplishing the tasks as the Captain indicated while Hans spoke. The Table and chair were already set up.

Hans Nodded sitting down, "That should get us started, Captain. Thank you."

A Command Tent was actually built around Hans. There was good news; miraculously there was a lower than five percent casualty rate. The bad news was Hans was the only Member of the command ranks that survived. Hans used chains of communication and rebuilt some form of governmental order. He set up a new council promoting six military commanders and appointing eight Civilians to the Council.

Word came in from the Caravan and Lord Rolland was welcomed to join in the rebuilding of Shadow Valley and Shadow Keep. Lord Rolland, two of his captains and two civilians from his people joined the Council. The tentative decision that those that came from the Barony of Pendril would make ShadowKeep their home, at least for a while was agreed upon. They focused on rebuilding the village first. A portion of the guards were pulled back to rebuild and maintain defenses. They had to watch disasters of this magnitude tended to cause bands of ruffians and cutthroats to prey on weak and if the bands get large enough even on villages and poorly protected keeps.

Stralina was put in charge of running the medical camp and it was quickly moved to the center of the Aura of healing created by the Ancient of healing. Stralina wondered if Bonny was going to come and join them. This was not restricted to their Valley though; she wondered what was behind it. A shiver ran down her spine; what darkness was distracting the Ancients with this calamity and what was it heading this way? This was not an attack; it was a decoy. An attack would have taken more lives.

*　　*　　*　　*　　*

Racken had been moving at a fairly fast clip and almost did not pull back fast enough to avoid plunging into the depths of the crevice that split the mother mountains. After that he moved much slower, traveling south looking for a way to cross the divide. He was forced to weave away and back and wanted to curse the slowdown in his progress to seek help. He considered the possibility he would not find a way to cross. He did not think the dwarfs of Darkalon would help him. The dwarf nation did not rate the Milmorg much higher than the Prak longtime enemies to Drakalon.

If he had to, he would go all the way south to the ocean, his lizard mount could swim the distance. The northern lizards they used for mounts did not like salt water and it was not really good for them, but in times like these you do what you have to do. A troll lumbering some distance ahead, howling some insane gutturals, pulled Racken's attention back to where he was. He pulled back and the lizard stopped, both of them watching the troll vanish and waiting until the ranting faded before proceeding. It was probably separated from troll hollow by the rip in the mountains and Racken had no desire to find out why it was howling in such a manner.

He proceeded forward paying more attention to the sounds of the land around him. Considering how his own people were so caught by the new cult, it could be even the tamest of encounters might not be what they seem. His lizard sensed his concern and darted from one place of cover to another, even traveling in a manner to help conceal their passage. There were places where the gap narrowed, but never seemed to be enough for him to have confidence that they could leap the distance. Having passed near enough to Troll Hallow to see a rampaging troll, they were within a day's travel of the flat lands, home of the Prak nomads.

Racken wondered if this split in the land followed the mountains, cutting through the Kingdom of Talmorg or if it traveled a different course. He realized he didn't know if he could even get to the Southern Ocean, this crack could circle around and lead him back north to his homeland. He had to find a way to cross.

*　　*　　*　　*　　*

Merlin was back in his room in the Walled City of Talmorg. Relatively speaking not much time passed while he was away, but now it was midday. The City of Talmorg had felt the earthquake, but the impact was not devastating. A few of his messengers had reported back, others would take as much as days to gather the information he asked of them. The small creatures of the land did his bidding when he asked them, they were his friends. The strange new religious orders were not trying to get a foothold in the major cities under the protection of the Ancients. Merlin pondered why. Perhaps whatever power they used was of no effect in protected areas, or perhaps they were avoiding detection and exposure by working from areas of less population first.

He finished lettering and signed the scroll he was working on and rolled it slipping it in the bundle with the rest. He needed to get the collection of reports to the appropriate members of the council. Times where shifting, he had to continuously reassess everyone he was dealing with. He had to watch for signs of who might slip into the influences of subversive efforts of hidden enemies. He kept himself under a minor glamor avoiding notice as he moved in and out. While he was free to move through any part of the kingdom he wanted as he pleased, he felt there was prudence in avoiding being noticed by any who would wish to track that movement. Besides it was fun to keep his fingers in the arts and to measure those around him for their abilities also.

Turning down the back street on the south side of the city he slipped into the closest thing to the underbelly in Talmorg. His business took him to all classes and types. Before the day was done, he would also find himself in the royal halls disclosing matters to King Talmorg and his son Prince Tamlorn.

*   *   *   *   *

Chareece stepped from the meeting to her bedroom. It was later than she meant to be back. She would just tell her dad that she spent time with Eric this morning. He would shake his head, nod, and go back to his business without asking any more questions. It was later in the day then she wanted it to be. After making sure she was alone in her room, with a gesture she changed into appropriate clothing to face the day.

As she stepped out of her room, the guard in the hallway greeted her. "Good morning, milady. Your father was by looking for you and asked me to send you his way when I saw you."

"Thank you Geldron" starting to turn towards her parent's quarters. The kingdom did not know Eric was her blood father.

"Milady," Geldron caught her attention again, "they are about the days business in the advisory chambers. The affairs of state must be attended to." He made a half gesture almost apologetic in the opposite direction from which she was headed.

"Thank you again, Geldron. You honor me with your patience." seeing the relief however minor at her not getting indignant and gracious acceptance of the messenger, she nodded and headed to meet her dad.

As she walked, she could feel Melina inside her. It felt good, even through the sense of guilt and sadness. It also somehow felt empowering. She would have to learn more about how to take care of her dedicated servant. She was registering that she was now completely responsible for this soul that had given itself willingly to her. Then she also wondered how much of everything she was doing was Melina aware of.

Pausing and looking out the window so as not to be conspicuous, Chareece built a room in her mind. She then focused on making a clean split of her attention. Chareece would go and talk to her parents and ShadowDancer would bring Melina into her chambers and learn more about what she was dealing with. When ShadowDancer first stepped into the room it was a simple cube empty and made of finished white marble.

Melina was in the room with her. "Hello, Melina." with a thought, chairs and end tables appeared.

Melina dropped to one knee, "For your glory, ShadowDancer."

"Please, you have no need to kneel before me here. Sit in a chair and let's talk a little." Chareece was not sure what she was doing but hoped that it did not show too much.

"You are most gracious." Adoration filled the young woman's eyes.

ShadowDancer was going to ask her age but knew the answer as soon as she thought to ask. "You were only 14 years of age, still new to life." she paused, stopping herself from planting regret in the young woman's thoughts. "Your sister is only 22, she too is young to be a priestess, but I am honored by the sacrifices both of you are making."

"To server our goddess is not a sacrifice, ShadowDancer," she seemed to stumble for a moment on what to call her, "it is an honor and a reward."

ShadowDancer realized this might be harder than she thought. She would need to be careful with the words she chose and the things she said. Chareece was not sure she was ready for this responsibility. Nodding to the words spoken by the young lady, "I wish for my people to live and help each other and to help those in need around them." With a thought ShadowDancer put a goblet of nectar and a plate of fruit and bread in front of Melina.

"Thank you," after another uncertain moment, she continued, "How do you wish I address you, my goddess?"

She thought for a moment, looking into the girl's eyes, almost half her own age, "For ease and comfort you can use milady, but in the presence of others ShadowDancer." This was not much different then how she was treated as Princess.

The girl smiled brightly and flourished a slight bow where she sat, "Yes, milady."

"Was there anything you expected to happen when you sacrificed yourself?" ShadowDancer hoped the uncertainty of her wording was not evident.

Melina tilted her head in thought and fondled a piece of fruit for a moment, "I guess, I expected to be no more myself, to lose my identity and become no more or less than a part of the power you wield. I only hoped that my loss would help bring your grace to my family and my people. I really did not expect to know my own thoughts again."

*   *   *   *   *

Chareece was a little surprised, as she continued through the hallways to meet with her parents in the throne room, at the ease with which she could keep her persona divided. She was aware of everything ShadowDancer was doing with Melina, but able to stay clear on who she was as Chareece. Her interactions with those she passed and spoke to, left no indication that a part of her was in a totally separate world having a calm conversation in a secluded room.

"Milady" The guards greeted her as she turned to enter the room behind the door in the hall, "His Majesty is expecting you."

"Thank you." she gave a slight nod of acknowledgment to both of the guards and headed into the hustling and bustling of the room.

*   *   *   *   *

Talmorg found himself waking up as he was shaken out of his bed. He reached out through the adoma, the magic life essence of the land granted them by Eric. An adoma was the life force found in the homelands of each of the races granted them by some of the Ancients, with one of the exceptions being human before Eric arrived in their world. Talmorg could feel that all the land around them had been shaken by a distant quake, but it was not so major here as to do serous damage to the kingdom.

"What was that?" Saphrine asked slipping out of the far side of their bed.

"An earthquake that is a long way off, but very powerful." Talmorg slipped into appropriate robes to make a public appearance. Saphrine was equally attired and at his side as they slipped from the room. "Captain, I'll need reports in the throne room as quickly as they can be gathered."

Shiheel and Hesheil were already at their places around the advisory table along with several other members. Talmorg noticed that Merlin had not yet arrived, perhaps the violent shaking was not enough to wake him. Some members of visiting councils were also in the meeting hall. This was going to be an interesting day. Saphrine sat on her throne beside him as he sat down.

"What do we know?" he asked openly to whomever had an answer.

At least half of those present were themselves still trying to wake up and gather their thoughts. Shiheel responded first as he almost always did, factual with no emotion reflected in his voice, "Even though it was a strong shock wave here, it seems to be from at least half the continent away. It seems to have come from the east, but my readings are a little confusing as if it were from everywhere east, or several different locations stretching to the north and south at the same time."

"What about our people?" Talmorg probed, "Are our people okay? If they are okay, what about live-stock, buildings? I need to know the state of the kingdom."

Messengers were slipping in and out. Elisorn, Lord of internal relations for the City of Talmorg, after quickly scanning a few reports, spoke up, "It seems so far we, our people have not been hurt, we have no more medical incidents reported then normal for this time of the day. Nothing unusual has been reported from inside the city yet. People seem to just be a little disorientated by the shake."

"That is good news. We need news from the rest of the kingdom now." Talmorg looked back to Elisorn, "Take what men you need to insure the well-being of the people of our city." Talmorg continued giving instruction and gathering information. Before they were done emissaries would be sent to every village and corner of the kingdom and after ensuring the state of the kingdom, they may send assistance to others beyond their borders that may need help.

A couple hours had passed when Chareece slipped into the room. Talmorg wondered where she had been but chose not to ask and put it out of his mind. "How can I help, Father?" she asked.

"Well, what we need right now is information. I need to know how the kingdom is doing and where they may need help, but it will take days for messengers to arrive from various villages. If they did not send any, it will take twice as long for our messengers to get to the locations and back."

"We have other ways of communicating afar, do we not?" she interrupted. "I have some resources I can use." She paused waiting for his answer.

"Anything you can learn will be helpful." Talmorg was not sure what she was talking about, perhaps she had gained more resources than he was aware of, this would be a good thing. She had led several efforts to assist the less fortunate of the kingdom over the past several years. "We do have winged messengers in route, but the amount of information they can carry is limited. I also have scryers looking to the distances they can reach."

Chareece started to speak but paused stunned for a moment that Melina had been so readily willing to let everything end for herself that her family might have some benefit. She forced herself back to her surrounding, but not before Talmorg got a concerned look on his face. "I apologize, I was just distracted for a moment there. I will go and see what my resources can find."

*　　　*　　　*　　　*　　　*

ShadowDancer looked at Melina and stood up. Windows appeared in the walls. "Come." She walked to the windows, "These are portals to view our people, those who call upon me or follow us. You can 'will' yourself to them and back here as my messenger. I want you to go to them to their villages and the places they live and report back to me everything you can about the aftermath of the quake."

"Yes, Milady."

"You do not need to appear to the people or talk to them. You may take a few minutes with your sister if you wish but be quick and return to me the information you can." ShadowDancer pushed her thoughts to Melina, hoping she would understand, it would be quicker than trying to explain. Melina smiled, bowed, went to one of the windows and vanished.

*　　*　　*　　*　　*

Chareece went off to an area in the room where a few of her handmaidens were waiting for her. She had a very real network of spies that kept her apprised of the affairs of the kingdom, but for now they were just a cover for her real source. She hoped she was not doing anything wrong, all she needed was to start getting reproved by the Ancients. What Gaharious said came to mind, 'you are not bound by the same rules as the Ancients' she was not sure if she was paraphrasing, but the gist was the same. This did not mean there were no rules, she was sure.

She wondered if she could split her own identity and actually be in different places at the same time. As if the thought brought it to pass, ShadowDancer was standing in front of Chareece and they were gazing upon each other and yet she was both. As fascinating as it was, she made ShadowDancer vanish. Chareece looked quickly around perchance who may have seen what happened, while ShadowDancer raced eastward to survey where the fault split the continent and see if the kingdom was in one piece.

Chareece was not sure, but if anyone had seen ShadowDancer, they were not making it evident. She realized she needed to be more careful if she was to avoid being detected. Melina called her, Chareece sat down, another split of her thoughts and ShadowDancer was in the room with Melina, but also still racing towards the fault unseen.

"Most are ok, Milady. There are some who have suffered a little, but your followers generally have less to lose then those around us." Melina began.

"Shh, let me see what you have seen." ShadowDancer touched Melina on the temple and all her journey was shared. "You have done well, but I need to go for a bit. Speak the things you desire while you are here, and I will take care of your needs." ShadowDancer vanished from Melina's presence.

Chareece took a deep breath, it was not as easy to maintain the third persona, maybe practice would help, but not right now. Wandering eyes glanced at her and looked quickly away as if not wanting her to see that they noticed anything. She stood up and headed back to the front table. ShadowDancer had just finished tracing the fault from the ocean halfway up the Mother Mountains.

Talmorg gave her an odd look as she walked up and picked up a quill and stepped over to the map of the south lands. "Chareece?"

"I am going to mark the exact location of the fault on the map, Father." She glanced at him before dipping the quill and beginning to mark the map, "Right now there is no reasonable passage other then taking a boat or ship around the southern end of the split. The heat from the molten flow will incinerate any attempts at building a wooden bridge. The continent is divided."

"How did you get this information?" General Calbork asked who stood watching as she divided the continent with a line from the tip of her quill. "We are days away from being able to confirm what you are telling us."

"I have my sources." She smiled a deep smile that would have melted almost anyone and added, "Don't you trust me?"

"My apology, Milady, it is not you I doubt. I am just amazed that you can gather such information so quickly."

Talmorg step up and spoke, "What about people? Do you know if there are places, we need to send help?"

"Zarco and Tarsha were hit hard, Morbin and the Forest of Dreams may also need some help. Other then that, we may want to increase patrols on the roads to protect from highwaymen trying to take advantage of the calamity for personal gain." Chareece felt the others staring at her and knew they wanted to know how she knew things.

"What help do they need?" Talmorg inquired further.

"Harmosk will need added medical supplies, and funds to help rebuild. Morbin and the Pixies may need assistance in some of their rebuilding. The further west you go from the crack, the less damage. The crack that caused the quakes here reaches from the North Pole to the South Pole. There is something coming that is much worse than the splitting of the world, there is more at stake then the south lands."

"Calbork, see to the aid being sent to the east." Talmorg looked at Chareece. The kingdom did not know, but he knew that her father was Eric, and she was born with the blood of the Ancients. It seemed that she had at least some ability from this. He was not certain he wanted to ask. He was grateful to have timely information about the status of his people.

Merlin Starnook entered the throne room and called Talmorg's attention. "We have urgent matters to discuss, Lord Talmorg.". He dropped a bag of scrolls on the table next to the map. He pulled out a couple scrolls as everyone patiently waited. "We are faced with worshipers of Jaharadan. There are scattered followers throughout the less populated parts of the kingdom. The religion seems to be coming from the north somewhere."

"Who is Jaharadan?" Chareece asked before Talmorg could get the question out. "Is he an ancient?"

"Last I knew he was not. I understood he died back around the time the Dark Council disappeared. He was a necromancer and sorcerer who was in service to the Dark Council. I can not tell if he is around or if he is actually dead, but it really doesn't matter at this point. He either is or someone else who has a bit of power is using his name and cults have sprung up all over worshiping him. Followers seem to be under some sort of mind control, so it is hard to tell if they chose to worship or are being made to worship."

"What is with the scrolls?" Talmorg asked.

"These contain the information I have thus far been able to obtain concerning this problem. I do not think it is unrelated to the quake and the other incidents that have been happening around the world. There have been reports of the dead rising, and skeletons moving around in formations." Various members gathered started reading through different scrolls sharing them as they were done.

Chareece gasped and everyone looked at her. "The Milmorgs to the north east of the Mother Mountains have almost all been converted to this new religion. There is one who escaped that is coming to us seeking help."

"How do you know this, where does this new wealth of information come from?" a frustrated bureaucrat in the crowd asked doubting what she said.

"ShadowDancer," she paused looking at Talmorg catching herself before she said the wrong thing, "told me. I have communed with her on and off for a while now and she seeks to help us."

Merlin attempting to pull the attention away from Chareece while considering what she previously said. He spoke a little louder than normal.

"This means the Prak, the Wonk and the other wandering tribes of the north are probably also effected."

Talmorg pulled Chareece to the side away from the conversation and away from hearing range of Saphrine her mother also. "You have brought us much information. You are hiding something from me, but at least for now I do not want to know. You need time to get control of what you are doing, take your handmaidens with you and let them be your messengers until your attention is better focused."

She knew he knew, but the time was not right for him to think about it. "Thank you, dad. I will send you news as I get it."

*   *   *   *   *

Racken paused looking at the fiery magma in the ravine below, the barrier that cut him off from the west, cut him off from hope. His progress was greatly slowed by returning to the edge and looking for possible ways of crossing. Perhaps he should just head for the ocean and accept that he will not be able to cross before he reaches the shore. As he was about to yield to the inevitable, a woman clothed in fire and shadows of fire appeared in front of him. He noted her elf features, the licks of flame and shadow keeping her sufficiently clothed for modesty's sake and her red hair falling back as flame and shadow itself. He was gripped by fear at her appearance, yet found her presence comforting and reassuring at the same time.

"You are Milmorg? What brings you here?"

"I am." He was unable to resist answering her, "I seek help for my people. A strange new religion has stolen their minds and has us preparing for war. The madness needs to be stopped."

"I am ShadowDancer, what is your name and where are you going?"

"My name is Racken and I seek to find aid. I was intending to go to the Uklian to seek help from the seat of Gaharias, but I have been forced much farther south by this rip in the land. I was thinking perhaps I might find help from his majesty in the Walled City of Talmorg, that it is perhaps not too late for my people, but this ravine blocks my passage." Racken wondered why he was just telling this evil looking beautiful seductress everything she wanted. Then he felt himself and his mount lift from the ground. He was awed as she led the way and set them down again on the other side of the ravine.

"Good speed to you, Racken." She waved, turned and vanished northward up the ravine.

Racken took a few moments to get his bearings. She had indeed taken him to the other side, it was not his imagination. He nudged his mount forward and his surroundings blurred with the speed of their movement. She had done something to them, and they were moving faster then he knew possible. Racken decided that ShadowDancer was not evil, but he did not know what she was.

He was not familiar with these parts, but was hoping that if he kept going southwest, he would find a road or someone who could direct him the rest of the way to the seat of the mixed elven kingdom. They raced through the forested mountains crossed a river and more mountains. He reigned to a stop when they reached a road going east and west through the mountains. The road had a light dust covering that seemed undisturbed save for the tracks of his mount. No one has passed either way since the shake that caused the great ravine.

He headed west, one way or another, this road would lead him to his destination. Racken did not stop to rest. He paused when they reached a fork in the road and fed his mount and ate from his rations. The signs indicated that to the West was Dragoncove and to the south was his destination, The Walled City of Talmorg.

*   *   *   *   *

Darval ordered a third of his legions to be readied to make the journey back to Ethar if he needed them. He had no vested interest in the affairs of Ethar, but Gaharias was still his brother and he still felt an obligation to his people that were left behind. Once he had given them the opportunity to return with him to the Shadow Realms, then he would be done with the meddling in the affairs of that world.

Alone in his meditation garden, Darval looked into the mirrors of his mind. He had remnants of people on every continent Ethar offered. It was time to check on them and open the opportunity to them to cross to the Shadow Realms. Those that chose to join him, really have no part in the wars that are impending on the old world. He started at the southernmost continent, covered mostly in the polar cap. Sending messages to the seers, word would spread quickly, they could talk and make their choices. Then he sent words to his people on the scattered islands and island continents offering them the choice. They had gone a time without his guidance, some choosing to follow after other Ancients, others holding fast to waiting for Darval's return.

From the island continent in the west, he reached across to the first major continent. It was here that he first started noticing some anomalous behavior. The impending affairs of Ethar were touching his people from the western cave dwellers to his winged minions in Deamorg there were scattered groups following after some new religions. This was not yet enough to set off any alarms, but he was concerned that the source of these factions was hidden from his normal knowledge of events around his people when he talked to them.

Alarms did go off in his mind when he got to the tribes on the north west corner of the continent directly south of the more recent activity that drew his attention back to Ethar. His people had formed tribes that were practicing necromancy and blocking him out so that he could not tell if there were any that still sought him. They had the same cult behavior he had seen barely starting up on the western continent. As with most dark art practicing tribes, there were a few priests controlling the thoughts and behaviors of the masses. Only those who were sold out to the practice were allowed the practice of free will. It also seemed to him that his people were the primary targets of whatever power was at work.

He pushed to the forbidden continent, expecting to find his minions there in slumber. They were up, focused and preparing for war. Their minds were under a spell and out of his reach. "for the time being" he whispered out loud. Darval grew angry.

*   *   *   *   *

Hans Spardic sat at the makeshift command post reviewing reports, issuing orders and instructions. Reports told him his wife and son were still running the medical camp, seeing to the healing of the sick and wounded. He took the time to go see them a couple of times, but time was pressing as they all recovered from the disaster. Casualties were not as severe as first estimated, but the hierarchy above him had all been removed. He was now the High Lord of ShadowKeep. He would receive the title 'HonorLord' at a ceremony sometime after things were settled down.

"The throne room is still standing secure, and debris has been cleared out." A Messenger reported.

Hans did not hesitate, "The command post will move to the throne room in 10 minutes, make ready. Send a Unit out to help those of Pendril with supplies and parts to help repair the rest of their caravan."

The temporary command post was packed and picked up and they were moving to the throne room as soon as the last messenger was sent back out to advise the other coordinating camps of the move. Repair and cleanup crews where already busy restoring the artifices that had been damaged. There was a lot of damage to the walls and parapets that had been built onto the mountain, but the core structure still stood solid carved out of the mountain itself.

Hans noted a few new cracks in the internal rock of the mountain. "We will have to send word to the Eftites in the Walled City of Talmorg and see if we can have a few come down and inspect and repair the stone of the mountain."

"Who is that my lord?" a Captain he was not familiar with asked.

Hans realized without much thought most of his people were not familiar with the peoples of the farther reaches of Ethar. "Sorry, I was thinking out loud. It is a matter I will attend to myself."

Evening approached as they settled into the throne room and activities were starting to, for appearance's sake at least, look more like normal business. Hans had placed a chair in front of the thrones at the base of the steps where he attended to the affairs of state as chaos moved towards order again.

Hans took leave, stepping into a side chamber, "first things first" he whispered to himself. He focused and with his mind he found Shiheel and whispered in his thoughts, "My friend, I need help re-securing the stone of the mountains at ShadowKeep. There is damage done by the quake and it needs repaired." He knew Shiheel would send a few of the Eftites to attend to his need.

"and now" he whispered, taking the amulet in his hand that he received from Eric. He stepped out once again in his living room. Someone was knocking at the front door. Without hesitation he used his power to change his clothing and opened the door. "Hello?"

Officer Terrell was a bit surprised to see him, "Jaffro Jaimes?"

"Yes, officer." he nodded.

"Would you mind coming downtown with me. The chief would like to see you himself. He thought you were dead." The officer turned and started back towards the car expecting Jaffro would follow. He did. The story he told the chief was that he was on an anthropology expedition and had only just returned. It was a surprise invitation, and he did not have time to let anyone know. He had committed no crime so after some questioning, the chief let him go. Officer Terrell drove him home left after he went inside.

While days had passed on earth, seemingly no time had passed when he returned to attend to business at ShadowKeep. He took advantage of the opportunity to return fully rested.

*　　　*　　　*　　　*　　　*

Jaharadan let loose a laugh with more evil then any Jahaln had previously heard. "So, you have happened upon an ancient dragon graveyard. These will do well to divide attention and instill fear in our enemies."

Jahaln looked upon the scores of winged skeletons, "How shall we use them to that purpose, my lord?"

Jaharadan had been etching a rough map of the world on the ground as he spoke, "We shall scatter them against all of the major cities of the world. The damage they do will be minor of no consequence, but they will force the eyes of defenders to watch the sky and not just the ground and their very existence will instill fear and doubt."

Jahaln nodded at the plan, "Some will be flying for quite a time to the farther reaches."

"Ah, we cannot have that." The liche calmly stated, "We will simply have to port them to the proximity. Besides we do not want forewarning from the neighboring villages."

Jahaln examined the knowledge he had and found in fact he knew how to cast spells that would port these creatures where he wanted them. He even knew coordinates that were in the general locations of the populated areas of the world. "Your gifts to me have been generous, may they serve you well."

"Let us begin, I will begin at the south and you begin from the north. The quake and this should keep things in turmoil long enough for us to organize the rest of our plans. Once we have established ourselves as a power in this world, they will be forced to accept us in the courts of the Ancients."

"Yes, my lord." As he sent his first bone dragon among the Jinn to the north. This is when Jahaln first realized Jaharadan was not after something as mundane as control of the world, he wanted to infiltrate the council of the Ancients. Perhaps his goals were even bigger than that. What they were doing, was no more than placing their game pieces and turning up the first cards in a much bigger game. Jahaln was a survivor and was already tapping into his new-found knowledge to build his escape routes and survival plans should they fail or succeed.

Methodically they sent out the bone dragons, these were not armies of war, they were in fact only to breed terror and fear. Fear added to the strength of the lich. Jaharadan seemed to gain more life, even a youthful appearance in a dark way as the harbingers of evil went forth performing their dark deeds.

*   *   *   *   *

Gaharias sat in his chair by the fireplace examining the floating orb in front of him. There were disturbances all over Ethar, but the enemy was still hidden. It was Jaharadan, this much he knew. He could gather that much from the scattered people of Darval that he tried to take care of in the absence of his brother. Some of his own people had also become aware of the return of the assistant to the Dark Council and wondered if this was a sign of their return.

The Uklian Elves saw the cult running like a disease through the scattered tribes to their east. They fortified and prepared to defend themselves. They were not afraid, but they also did not know the scope of what was happening. Even after the war that made them allies with the south lands, they chose to stay isolated from the world outside their own kind.

Gaharias had elf adomas on other continents, and they were friendlier with their neighbors, but the Uklian were unique and probably the most powerful of the elf races he called his people. He added as much strength as he dared. He didn't want any sudden change to draw the attention of the other Ancients and have them questioning his actions. Although he was less careful in increasing the number of Avatars he empowered for their loyalties.

He needed to call a meeting of the Ancients of Ethar and let them know that trouble was stirring, and their races may need them. He hoped Trelldin Darkolon ancient for the dwarf people of the southlands to the east would help protect the continent. This event was all over Ethar, he hoped all of the council would step up and help protect their people. He hoped that they would work together towards this end. Gaharias knew though, that there would be division, and some would see this as an opportunity to try and grab more power while others would turn their back. Some of the Ancients had already abandoned Ethar and their people, *"We cannot walk among them, why should we care?"*. They chose instead to build their own private worlds each in their ethereal providence outside of the boundaries of Ethar.

Gaharais used his indirect powers to encourage his peoples around Ethar to build defense and make allies. He could not directly act on the course of events, nor was he allowed to ask others to directly act on his behalf. He did what he could without overstepping at least not seriously the limits placed on him by treaty.

*   *   *   *   *

Lord Valdir felt helpless as he watched himself and Balgrin ordering their minions to the boats. The fleet was massive, they had been building ships in secret for years, hiding them in the rocky crags of the coast. Their newfound master hid from them and had no regard for their races or survival. Everyone old and young was armed and ready for war. This is not war, he thought, this is destruction. War you prepare to win, not just to kill

'I still have free thought, even if it is deep and separated from the control over what I am doing and saying.' He had hope that he might find a way to overcome what controlled them. He only hoped it would be before it was too late. 'Darval where are you? Your people need you.'

Valdir wondered if Balgrin still had an inner detached self that was fighting the same battle he was. From the occasional looks it was a possibility. Valdir started trying to push thought to his conscious mind, if nothing else perhaps he might cause distractions and slow down the events he otherwise had no control over. He started pushing images of weapons stored in the mountains that he knew were not real. He pushed strings of unrelated thoughts, in hopes of finding a chink in this inner armor.

'Time will find a weakness and I will regain control.'

Balgrin also was brooding in his mind. He realized that if whatever was controlling them did not have something specific, they were doing, he could sometimes look where he wanted or make lesser movements that were not seemingly important. He could not take any decisive actions, at least not yet, but minor thought actions, like scratching an itch   Perhaps they were not all effected the same. He had at least a place to start working against that which controlled them.

*   *   *   *   *

Stralina was relieve that they had taken care of the worst cases and things were settling down. There were not that many injured considering. Darvarias was still busy attending to routine injuries now, and they had both relinquished most of the non-critical care to the rest of the medical personnel that had joined them. Houses had been rebuilt from what was salvaged over the last few days and while shared they gave place for shelter and rest. "I am going to go around and check everyone again Darvarias, then I think we can rest for a bit and let others do their part."

Darvarias nodded, "I am hungry too. We should take time to eat."

Things were not as bad as they could have been, but there was still some sobbing for lost ones and the need for vigilant attendance to those who were not yet on the comfortable side of surviving. The will of the individual to survive does have effect on their healing, so loved ones were encouraged to spend time with the recovering.

Stralina was thankful for the brief interludes she had with Hans between being pulled back apart by their obligations to the people. Word had come that the central command had been moved to the throne room and she knew that Hans was now High Lord by default. She should go join him. With a nod she summoned a banquet on a table by the Medical camp sufficient for all to eat heartily.

"Darvarias it is time for us to return to the keep." something inside her felt a heavy sadness, but she brushed it off as a side effect of the disaster.

Darvarias joined her, "Things will be okay again, mom." but a tinge of sadness caught him off guard as she placed her hand in his arm and they started towards the keep.

One of the guardian dragons bellowed high on one of the precipices of ShadowKeep. As the two of them looked up there was this awful cracking thud. Stralina heard it more than felt it as she looked down and saw the bone fragment piercing her garments above her left breast. There was thudding and a couple screams of pain around them somewhere. Stralina clung to her son's arm and looked him in the eyes. "I love you." with a slight gasp of pain she added, "Tell him I love him too." Her eyes closed the darkness a welcome relief to the pain.

"Mom, NO!" Darvarias fell to his knees holding his collapsed mother as if the very act of holding her would bring her back. The light was gone, no magic he knew no medical training could repair her pierced and ripped heart from the splintering bone. The charred remnants of the bone dragon fell to the ground not far away, but it was too late. His own heart felt as if it had been ripped inside where nobody could see it. He had no time to prepare, no warning. After a time, he let her slip through his arms and a numbness crept over him. He must tend to her last wish, he had to go to his father and tell him. Soldiers he had not seen come up helped him to his feet and lifted Stralina from the blood that pooled on the ground. They were guided and carried to the shelter of the keep.

*   *   *   *   *

Eric and Bonny stepped through together to Ethar. The room they stepped into was set aside for them to use. It was in the palace, Talmorg had decided it was not best for them to randomly appear in open public places unless that was what they intended to do. The room had all of their accommodations. It was actually part of a suite of rooms reserved for them. There was a computer in the corner and there were other things that they had set up to help them with their tasks as Ancients on Ethar.

Bonny stepped over to the large crystal orb that helped her observe events around Ethar. She was sensitive to healing needs and her observations through the crystal were drawn to those places where the need was the greatest. "The injuries from the cracking are not as bad as I would have expected."

"I do not know where we will be needed or what we will be doing yet. Perhaps we should look more where our attentions are not being called. We may learn more looking in the places where the calls to the Ancients have gone silent."

Bonny noticed Eric was right, there were areas where requests had gone silent. "I see what you mean, every continent has at least one section that is quiet to us." She focused in on one and then another. At first, she did not see anything unusual, but then, "They seem empty. I mean the people look healthy enough, but their movement looks mechanical and unattached, almost like they were zombies."

"They are not acting under their own will." Eric added.

A commotion stirred outside. Eric was at the window first and saw the bone dragon spewing arrow like bone fragments towards the city below. Bonny reached out and shielded the area below from the majority of the rain, but some got through before she saw what was happening. The guardians of the city took the creature down quickly and the event was over. They both looked at each other, they knew this was happening in the populated areas around the entire world.

"These are not acts of war," Bonny stated, "they are terrorist acts intended to divert attention from what is actually happening.

"We need to go say hello to Talmorg and Saphrine, then it will be time to meet again in the shadow realm to discuss what we have learned and make plans."

The guards in the hallway greeted them as they went out and headed towards the throne room.

CHAPTER 4

Ripples of power

ShadowDancer followed the great ravine to the northern glacier. The ravine kept going north, but she chose to go east, hidden with shadow and riding the wind. She passed through the high desert of the Jinn and over the eastern split of the mother mountains into the land of the Milmorg. As she passed through their towns and villages, they all seemed to be mindless followers of their newfound religion. She found none that were left unturned.

As she approached the city of Kalridan in the middle of the United City States of the Rackenwolf, she came upon a gathering in a field just outside the gates of the city. Still hiding in the shadows, she slipped to the center of the gathering to see what had their focus. There was what appeared to be a priest in robes and a cowl that hid his face standing over an altar. Several of the younger women of the village were there also robed across from the priest in front of the alter on their knees.

"For Jaharadan who has given us all things, we sacrifice that which is precious that we may live in his bounty and serve his will." the priest was finishing what he was saying.

One of the young Milmorg in the middle stood up and dropped her robe, "I give myself a sacrifice to Jaharadan upon his alter, that he should return his greatness and power to our people." She laid herself upon the alter. ShadowDancer noticed her voice seemed to have a flat tone and her actions seemed mechanical. She knew what was going to happen next. She caught the moment, time stopped. The dagger this priest held looked much the same as the priest who had infiltrated her people, a wavy sacrificial dagger and a soul stealer. She touched the young Milmorg that lay on the alter and pulled her out of herself.

"Who are you, young one?" she asked.

"I am Jeyra." she turned uncertain and saw herself laid out on the alter. "Who are you and what is happening?"

"Some call me ShadowDancer. I have caught you in a moment to learn from you why you are sacrificing yourself to this Jaharadan?"

She looked at ShadowDancer fear evident in her eyes. "I am not. I have no choice. I was forced to drink from a cup containing a warm salty bittersweet drink. Since then, I have watched myself through a fog. I do not even know what I am doing most of the time."

ShadowDancer felt for the Milmorg. She touched Jeyra's arm again and sensed the poison in her blood as she lay on the alter. After sensing it in the young woman, she could sense it in the other Milmorg around her with the exception of the priest. It seemed the priest was a willing participant. "Jeyra, I cannot save your life, but I can take you so that dagger cannot draw you to the evil purposes of Jaharadan. I can give you a choice to serve me for a time, or release you, or you can return to your body and the dagger above you shall draw you out for Jaharadan."

"If there is any way that I can help free my people, take me."

"I cannot be certain we can help, but we can try. I make no promises."

"If there is even a chance, I can be of help to them, she gestured out to her people, take me to serve you."

"Step into me of your own and be free to depart when you decide your time is done."

The spirited form of the Milmorg stepped into ShadowDancer and was drawn in. The taste and feel of taking them in was as good as the first time, even the surge of power. Part of her wished it was not so intoxicating, part of her wanted more and that scared her a little. She noticed there was a collection of skulls at the base of the alter and cups to pass the blood of the sacrifice to the gathering. Jeyra was dead before the dagger would reach her, would this change the outcome of the ritual?

ShadowDancer backed away from the crowd and observed from a distance. As before the soul stealer turned on the wielder the crowd was uncertain what to do, then some grabbed the ritual goblets, dipped them in the bowl of blood and drinking a sip passed them back to others in the crowd. The crowd disbursed in a less then orderly fashion and while they still had a glazed look in their eyes, she had a sense that the control over them might be slipping if only a little.

She headed south moving as fast as light through the Rackenwolf into the Morkin Flats. When she approached the villages, she slowed down to observe, which ones may have been effected by this ritual and which had not. It seemed there had to be a priest who served willingly for approximately every one-hundred-twenty poisoned followers. This was an important weakness.

As she passed through the nomadic lands of the Prak, she came upon another alter with a goblet still containing fresh blood. She grabbed it, putting a seal over the top. This she would give to Shiheel and Hesheil to see if they could create a counter agent, something to cure those that are infected, or poisoned. With a thought she was back in the court room with Chareece. The handmaidens stepped back at the appearance of ShadowDancer. Chareece requested that they leave the room for a few minutes. She pulled herself back together with a sigh of relief.

It was fun being able to be in two places at once, but it was a strain also. ShadowDancer separated again into the room inside her mind with Melina and pulled Jeyra in with them. This was much easier then being in different places in the world outside.

Chareece called her handmaidens back in. She wrote out a note on a scroll and sealed it with her personal signet ring, handed the scroll and the sealed cup of blood to Liyenna one of her handmaidens. "Please take these to Shiheel straight away."

She did not feel like writing out everything that ShadowDancer had seen, so she reached into a leather satchel she had at her side and pulled out maps and reports that she created as she reached into the bag. "Cercia," her handmaiden stepped up, "please take these to father."

"Milady" she bowed her head and followed Liyenna out of the room.

She wrote out another message concerning Racken and handed it to Tereline, "Take this to the Captain of the guard at the front gate."

This left one more handmaiden, Shylina, alone with her in the room. "Do we have any news yet from Efra?"

"Our agents sent word. There are no signs of this new cult following, but a remnant of a party of dwarfs from Darvish were sent on to here with an escort yesterday. A dwarf bard and his wife. The cracking split the ground where they were camped, and they do not know if the rest of their party was cut off on the other side or lost in the ravine. They were part of an emissary group that was being sent to improve relations between kingdoms of the east and west."

"I am going to need to depart for a little while soon. Please cover for me while I am gone. I will go to my room and leave from there, so you can tell everyone I went to my room for a bit." Chareece knew that their group was to gather again in the Shadow Realms soon and was making preparation. She even recreated documents with all the information she had thus far acquired inside her satchel. Her Father Eric would be there, she thought as she closed the door to her room. The thoughts of wonder about his home surfaced in her mind, it took her a moment to realize what happened.

She speculated she was in her Father's home. The walls and building around her were different than any wall she was familiar with, even the furniture seemed foreign to her. There were lights in the ceiling that did not burn and odd devices on the counters and walls that she did not recognize at all. She did not have time for this right now, she needed to get back for their meeting. With a thought she was back in her bedroom.

*　　*　　*　　*　　*

Darval arrived just after Darvarias finished telling Hans the ill-fated news and they were both in tears in a side room off the throne room when he entered. He knew what happened even had the guards not told him on the way in. "I am so sorry Hans." Darval set aside the anger that brought him here, although the news of what happened here added to that fire. "We need you here with us my friend. I wish I could go back and change what has happened. We are not perfect; we just do the best we know to do." He placed his arms around the father and son hoping he might add some comfort.

"Thank you, Darval." Hans said pulling himself back together.

"We all have our own ways of coping with what we have lost." Darval did not want to overstep, but added, "You know you can take as much time as you need." He caught the moment for the three of them, "and return without losing any time here. Darvarias, you also are able to do this. There is much I can teach you when you are ready. For now, if you need time to get away and come to terms with events, I will help you with that also."

"I will remember my mother and honor her. The cause of our people was her cause to. I will honor her in this." Hans nodded when Daravarias finished.

"It is time for me to accept the title of HonorLord, High Lord of Shadow Keep. These people will need reassurance that I am here for them in spite of personal loss."

They walked out of the room together. Hans addressed the room, "Put the word out; We will have the ceremony to declare our new High Lord in one hour. We will let Lord Rolland preside in recognition of he and his people joining us as a part of ShadowKeep."

There was a cheer around the hall and several people left in different directions. Darval waved someone over and a tall Dark Elf walked up. "This is Narcole battle master of the dark elves." Hans looked closely at Narcole, his skin had a layer that looked almost albino in translucence covering a black oily under-layer. His features like other elves were very much human features that were sharpened, ears appearing pointed, generally like someone sharpened, ears appearing pointed, generally like

like someone sharpened the edges of everything. Darval continued "We have opened passage between ShadowKeep and the shadow of ShadowKeep in the Shadow Realms. Because of events that have been revealed to me, I am ready to help fight and take a stand for the future of Ethar and the future of my people in the ShadowRealms. Narcole and his armies will fight with you when the time is right." Darval beckoned and lead the other three through hidden chambers and secret passageways of ShadowKeep. They spiraled down through chambers Hans, already knew about and then deeper through levels he did not think were there before.

"This is it," Darval stated, "The point where you actually pass from one realm to the other as you step through this door."

There were stairs that still lead downward in the continuing spiral. Hans sensed the magic set to misguide those who were not supposed to be here. They stepped through the door and found themselves in an identical reproduction of what they just stepped out of.

"Are you building a copy of Ethar?" Hans asked.

"Not exactly. The Shadow Realms form what we call shadows of other realms that touch them. There is not too much of a shadow of ShadowKeep here yet, the link has not been here long. It will grow the longer the link exists."

As they stepped out of the hidden chamber that led to the passage way, it was more like stepping into a ruin of ShadowKeep. There were a few partial walls, then they were outdoors in a dark jungle like environment.

"The dark elves live a short distance north of here. Do not be alarmed if you see ghost like images of people moving around, sometimes you can see shadows of the people in the adjoining realm. For now, we need to get back for your coronation. We will have time for questions later."

Hans was thankful for the brief distraction from events, but he was still heavy and ached that Stralina would not be there for this event. He followed the others back in, but just before he stepped through the door, the moment was caught. The others all stood still. He looked around because he did not think he did this and there was Stralina standing behind him.

"I cannot hold this long, Hans. I love you too, but you have to let me go. You have power now and while you cannot bring me back, the strength of your will is not letting me move on either. Beginning or end, love me enough to let me go."

He reached out and caressed her cheek; it was as real as it had ever been. He leaned forward and kissed her softly and she kissed him back. "I am sorry my love, I will let you go." He felt inside himself the release and a burden lifted with the letting go, but it still left a sadness behind for what he had lost. They let go of their kiss.

"Thank you."

He watched her fade as she glided back away from him.

Hans turned back to the door and started stepping through again, as he did, time returned to normal. He looked at his son and wondered if she would give him closure also. Darvarias looked back and nodded as if he had heard the thought. It occurred to him, if he was an ancient, then so was his son Darvarias. How much power was his son manifesting and has he been hiding it behind Jinn magic. Hans decided that he would ask this in private at a later time, for now they had much work to do. Another thought crossed his mind, he was kinda like Aries the Greek god of war and he wondered if the Greek gods were a crossover of a dimensional rift. Perhaps he would pursue archeology back on earth and see if he could get some answers.

They entered the throne room together. The audience was beginning to fill the chamber. Hans went to the head of the room and sat in the chair he had placed in front of the throne. He would not violate tradition by sitting in the throne before he was crowned.

Lord Rolland stepped up with an appropriate nod or bow of the head, "You do me an honor to allow me to preside over this occasion, especially when we have the company of an ancient." He glanced towards Darval.

"This is a matter for the people of Ethar not the Ancients. He is here on other business that is also urgent to us." Hans looked around the room, and then back at the two thrones behind him. He looked at the throne that would remain empty at least for now and whispered, "I hope to prove worthy."

Lord Rolland clap his shoulder, "I am sure you will. To me you have already proven yourself." Hans nodded accepting the man's assurance, even though they were talking about different things.

The ceremony was simple and had a morale boosting effect throughout ShadowKeep and the protected township. There was celebration and festivity. About two hours later, HonorLord and Darval excused themselves and parted for the meeting place in the Shadow Realms.

CHAPTER 5

Hide and Seek

Merlin Starnook approached the steps of the palace, a sack of scrolls slung over each shoulder and a satchel hung at his side. He was not stopped or questioned with his coming and goings even without using magic to hide his passage. He was known and a friend of the kingdom and the business he was about was usually important to the realm. The outer courts had rooms and pools that were open to public use, meetings held here were not private, nobody was forbidden to any of these areas, unless they were under threat of attack. Things grew more formal and restrictive, the deeper you went.

He entered the throne room and went straight to the information gathering section of the command tables. He handed various scrolls to different members of the task force gathered around and simply placed others in their proper places on the table. He looked up and watched as Eric and Bonny entered the room and went straight to Talmorg. They talked for a few moments and Eric deliberately looked back at him and nodded. Perfect timing, he walked into a side chamber and pulled out the amulet Darval had given him.

Eric and Bonny finished giving Talmorg reassurances, including providing various supplies that appeared in different side room using their special talents. They were recognized as Ancients, so it was their privilege to disappear and appear anywhere they chose. After releasing a final handshake, they vanished into the Shadow Realms.

* * * * *

Gaharias was frustrated that he let his hand be so tied by the treaty of the Ancients. The Old Ones had convinced him it was the right thing to do, and it did in fact end a long string of meaningless wars and gave the people of Ethar an opportunity to grow and work out their own peace. Now though they needed protection from dark forces and his hands were tied. He was not allowed to take any direct major action in the course of events. Many of the other Ancients face with this frustration had turned away from Ethar and gone off to start their own worlds.

Gaharias did not let go, he still cared about his people. He took a breath; he was doing what he could. He nurtured the strength of the adomas for his people again. He encouraged and inspired people to do the things that would help them when events started to unravel. Beyond that, he had to rely on the new Ancients and his brother who had not signed the accord. Chareece one of his heirs not bound by the treaty acting as ShadowDancer was able to do what he could not, and she was acting for the people.

Gaharias walked around his personal fortress. He was one of the first of the ancients to recognize the people of the world as more than just toys for them to play games with. Gaharias did not need the space, nor did he need the accommodations for cooking and other creature comfort, but they brought back the memories of his own family so long ago. There was a time when he had a wife and kids, and they were the most important things in his world. His wife had been a human from earth. His relationship was frowned upon and it was his eldest son that had gone back there before the worlds separated again to their own dimensional places. Eric was born of that lineage, a son several generations removed.

His second son had died in an old battle between Ancients for things that seemed to no longer matter. His wife under his protection lived a very long life, but eventually her mortality caught up with her. He had thought about filling his house, about building a world around it, but he still had races on Ethar that called to him and looked to him for guidance. Maybe he will make an outside and start a garden and entertain a few animals. For now, his focus would stay on his people on Ethar. It was time to meet the others in the Shadow Realms. Perhaps he should move there with his brother and take his people with him if they wish to make the move. Or perhaps he should expand his world here and bring a portion of his people here. He stepped through to the meeting place.

*   *   *   *   *

They were gathered again in the ShadowRealms. Darval had a table and chairs with food and drink. Chareece came as ShadowDancer, clothed only in fire and shadow, a vision no mortal could resist. Almost everyone had a collection of documented information that they brought with them. Gaharias took it upon himself to preside and the rest acquiesced. Bonny was not there at the first gathering, but she was there with Eric now.

"Has anyone located the nemesis leader or confirmed his identification?" Gaharias asked taking a sip from the goblet in front of him.

"It is Jaharadan." ShadowDancer stated plainly, "He infects or poisons the blood with something that takes away free will. It is delivered through a drink, that I think is made from the blood drawn in a ceremonial sacrifice. I noted he seems to need a willing priest to lead every hundred twenty followers, possibly because they need to drink from a daily sacrifice."

"Is that confirmed or rumor?" Gaharais looked at her carefully.

"I was there at a sacrifice; you know how you know things about what is happening? I knew it was Jaharadan. I stopped time." she paused, "I drew the sacrifice out of herself before she was pierced by the soul stealer dagger. Even though I had watched her place herself on the alter she told me she was not in control. She had lost control, and everything was a fog since the time they had made her drink blood from a goblet. Something happens to the blood from the alter when it is taken with those daggers. It puts the imbiber in a death like state susceptible to necromantic control. I have Shiheel and Hesheil working on an antidote or antiserum from a sample I took."

"It seems he has not been asleep all these years or dead as we thought." Darval added, "He has targeted those who were my people that were left behind. I do not believe he anticipated my return. Attempts I have made so far have not released anyone from this mind control. I have been working careful and from a distance."

Eric swallowed the small piece of fruit he was eating and observed, "So we know who, but we do not know from where. We know that he has found a way to influence people on every continent and we have identified one method he is using to gain his control, but we still need to find a way to stop it."

Everyone paused looking at Eric. Merlin broke the silence, "That about covers it. We do have a pretty good idea where armies are being built." He proceeded to spread out a map of the northern polar continent. Others started pulling out various documents they brought with them.

Eric whispered to Bonny and she produced a large blue orb over the table and Eric started transferring the information from their documents to the floating globe of Ethar. ShadowDancer immediately adopted what he was doing and poured her information onto the globe. The rest followed suite.

When everyone was done, Eric touched the globe, "Now we know where Jaharadan is not." The majority of the world glowed green. "This at least narrows the scope of where he might be. We also know where Jaharadan has at least some of those he has control over." Sections of the globe glowed red. "Jaharadan served the dark council, do we know where he operated from when he worked for the council, were there favorite places that he hung out?"

Darval raised an eyebrow, "These are the places he most commonly operated from." Neon blue spots appeared on the globe, "Probably the best places to start looking" that seemed to settle that matter, each taking note of places they could search. "Do we need someone else to examine the blood sample to search for an anti-dote?"

"I trust the Eftites." Eric stated.

"They will get the job done." Gaharaias added.

Eric looked at ShadowDancer "How are you keeping your dual identity hidden and still gathering information for Talmorg?"

ShadowDancer giggled, "It really is quite easy to prove I am not ShadowDancer." she stood up and Chareece stepped out of ShadowDancer.

There was another long silence. "I have never seen that done before." Gaharias stated

"I never thought to try." Darval added

Chareece shrugged, "Nobody gave me a rule book, so I just do things. I discovered this of necessity."

"Just like the room inside my mind," ShadowDancer added, "where Melina and Jeyra stay."

"Jeyra?" Eric raised both eyebrows.

"Yes," ShadowDancer answered "the young Milmorg I saved from the sacrificial soul stealer dagger the priest of Jaharadan was using."

"So, you have two servants now" Merlin asked almost apologetic.

"Not exactly, she is working with me, in hopes that she can help her people find freedom from Jaharadan's power. She is free to move on whenever she chooses. She did not give herself to me, I interceded with her permission, to save her from the fate of that dagger."

"Would you ask her to come before us, perhaps answer a few questions?"

"Sure." as she spoke Chareece brought Jeyra out, "These are friends Jeyra …" Jeyra was bowing to Darval before she could finish what she was saying.

"Milord" Jeyra prostrated herself before Darval.

"Rise up my child." Darval commanded and Jeyra stood with total awe in her eyes as she faced her ancient.

She glanced back at ShadowDancer with a moment of uncertainty. "I did not turn from you, Milord."

"Do not be afraid, you did well in accepting protection from my niece. Would you be so kind as to answer any question we may have concerning recent events." More of a statement then a question. "Please sit with us." as he gestured a chair appeared at the table for her to sit.

She sat and bowed her head, "I am honored."

Merlin spoke up, "Could you just tell us in your own words, what you saw happen to your people?"

Jeyra relayed her account of events. She told them "A strange religious group that started forming. Their ideas were so strange giving credit for everything to someone named Jaharadan, claiming he created everything, and he was the power behind everything. Most people just ignored them or avoided them, but it seemed that anyone who talked with them alone or went to one of their gatherings became one of their followers. When you talk to them, it was like they could not hear anything you said that disagreed with what they were doing. Then as their numbers grew it was noticed that people seemed to start disappearing. Rumors started that they were sacrificing people, but the government and the law were all under their control and nothing was done. Finally, they started forcing people to drink from their goblets. After they made me drink everything became a thick fog, I could not even tell what I was doing most of the time."

"Do you know what was in the goblet you drank?" Merlin asked

"I did not when I drank it, but ShadowDancer let me know it was blood. Seeing the way the gathering she took me from drank my blood from the alter I am sure it was." shame lowered her continence.

Darval put his hand on hers on the table, "Do not be ashamed, you have not done anything wrong here, nor have your people. This is the work of someone very evil." He glanced at ShadowDancer, "Perhaps you should return to your rest for now."

She stood up and bowed. Jeyra appeared to turn into a wisp of smoke as ShadowDancer drew her back in. Chareece merged back into ShadowDancer. "It is definitely easier to maintain one presence."

"How do you do that?" Bonny asked, "It looks like it might be quite useful."

"Well, the first time I did it, I built a room in my mind for Melina and projected ShadowDancer in there to talk with her. While I was busy as Chareece and I was talking with Melina as ShadowDancer, I had to answer a call as ShadowDancer, so I just left the room and was in two places at once. Then I, Chareece needed information from Melina while I, ShadowDancer was investigating the Ravine and I projected another ShadowDancer into the room with Melina. I noticed that the more places I was at once the harder it was to maintain."

"I was going to wait until I was in private to try myself. There have been many times in the past when I have wished I could be in more than one place at the same time." Gaharias stated.

"I think it and it happens." ShadowDancer stated plainly Chareece appeared.

"Then with a thought, I am one again." Chareece added and vanished.

"I can be whichever identity of myself I want to be or pull back from which ever part I want."

Bonny didn't say anything, she was wearing her Ethar outfit, and then there was another copy of her standing at her side wearing her earth clothing. "It works she said casually." She faced herself and each identity seemed to act independently, then she was just one again. "I am both, but one at the same time."

There was a long pause, then Eric turned to Hans, "We are all sorry about your loss. If there is something we can do to help." He left the statement open as a hanging question. Everyone nodded their sympathy.

Hans looked at Eric and held back his feelings, "She would want us to save the world, there will be time for mourning when that is done." Hans deliberately turned away and looked at Gaharaias, "You are the elder present, do we have a plan of action?"

Gaharais looked at the globe of Ethar floating between them, "We divide the world into areas that we will each search and watch for Jaharadan and alert the others if and when we find him. He is cloaking himself the way the Ancients do when they do not wish to be found by each other. He had to have learned that from time spent with some of us, who knows what else he learned. We also have to address the events he has started around the world. We can not only count on finding him to put an end to all this. What he has started will have at least in part have ongoing consequences with or without him. ShadowDancer and Merlin, the two of you already have the Northern Polar continent to search. Hans, you have the one you are on and you can also watch over the island continents to the north and south. Darval you have interests in the forbidden continent. I will search the other middle continent and the southern polar continent. Eric and Bonny, you can help anywhere you choose. You have powers that have not been fully explored that by far exceed my own. You will know more of what you can do then I. We are all working together, so everyone helps each other as you can. These are not limits that we know, these are just places to start to be sure we cover it all."

"I have remnants of my people on every continent," Darval hastened in, "I do not wish them any more harm than need requires. It is not by their choice they are being used for this evil cause."

"We will do what we can," Hans stated, "But war is not fair or just, if it were it might be the first option for resolving things."

"I am going to send a couple of my people through to try and assist Shiheel and Hesheil with that counter for the mind control." It was not clear which was stronger, Darval's concern for his people or anger at Jaharadan using them as if they were his own.

"We have a plan. We will communicate with each other as we discover anything and meet again here as needed." Gaharias closed the meeting. They all departed their separate ways. ShadowDancer changed to Chareece an returned to her room. Merlin returned to his office in the city of Talmorg. Hans returned to ShadowKeep. Eric and Bonny also returned to the Palace in the city of Talmorg.

"Things are changed brother." Darval said to Gaharias.

"It is not our world anymore. I am limited in what I can do, and you have a new world that has become your home."

"You can still join me."

"Perhaps, but this really is at least partly our mess to clean up." Gaharias looked hard at Darval, "You really should still answer when people of Ethar call to you, at least some of the time."

"I am answering this time." Darval looked at the globe still hanging over the table, "They are also family and we don't have to abandon them. You are right, I should have been answering."

*   *   *   *   *

Hans went up to the highest parapets of ShadowKeep to talk to the dragons that lived there. They protected ShadowKeep and ShadowKeep protected them, a bargain that had been in place long before Hans had come there to live. They were his friends too. There were often times when he would come up here just to talk with the dragons about anything. They had a different perspective no matter what you talked about.

"Greetings, friend, HonorLord," Drakalon rumbled, "I regret that we did not see that bone dragons sooner, we too shall miss Lady Stralina."

"Thank you, old friend. I do not lay her death at your feet. I blame he who sent the mischief. This in fact is why I am here, as much as I would wish otherwise, I have a favor to ask."

"We have served together and have been friends long enough, I am sure we will do what we can." Drakalon transformed into his human form to make conversation easier.

"That bone dragon was sent by a liche, Necromancer and who knows what else he is capable of, named Jaharadan. The bone dragons were just an intimidation tactic or something, perhaps a distraction. Jaharadan is amassing armies around the world. He is using secrets of the Ancients to conceal where he is from the Ancients, so we are searching everywhere. Will the dragons of ShadowKeep help in this search?"

"If the Ancients cannot find him, how can we?" Drakalon somehow did not seem totally sincere in his question.

Hans, HonorLord chuckled, "Line of sight. What magic cannot see from a distance; the eyes can still look upon. I will have to look everywhere again, but I was hoping you might be able to patrol the continent and the islands to the north and south and let me know if you see anything out of the ordinary."

"That is a simple request and a chance for us to stretch our wings. It will be our pleasure."

"Is there anything I can do for you to show my appreciation?"

"I will take that offer in the future. For now, friend, find your center again so that you will be ready for what is to come." Drakalon took a step backward, "Until next we talk, HonorLord."

HonorLord watched Drakalon leap up and transform back to a dragon. Over half the dragons took to the air, gathered briefly around Drakalon and then they all vanished in different directions. Drakalon was right, he needed to gather his focus, HonorLord, High Lord of ShadowKeep would need it. He descended through the maze through passageways others could not see and emerged in his office.

Donning his polished black armor, the Ebony Warrior now also HonorLord, he went to the fountain garden in the inner court to have some time to himself. He sat on one of the stone benches cross legged and gazed into the water falling through the tiers of stone to the basin below. His thoughts were clearing his breath taking an even rhythm and a courier called him entering the courtyard.

"My lord, some dockets need your approval."

He read through the papers, signed, and returned them to the courier, "Thank you. You may take them back."

After he was done with his third interruption, he whispered to himself, "I need a place to myself for a short time." The amulet pressing against his chest stirred with energy, he felt it merge with him, become a part of him as it activated. He was still in the fountain garden in the courtyard, but he has shifted dimensional plains and it seemed he had created a partial replica on the side of a hill with wooded thicket and there were only a few walls and pillars to the keep. He realized that he had taken on the form of a very large black dragon. It was a dragon amulet, he quickly transformed back to HonorLord. He sat for a good while; he mourned, wept and stared into the fountain. Some of the pain slipped away into the water, some seemed to grow a thicker skin and some washed away with his tears.

He stood and looked through the pillars at the other end of the garden and the ground seemed to drop away. In the distance he could see the expanse of plains on a world he did not recognize. He explored the edges of his garden island. He had created a copy of the gardens in a point between dimensions. As he looked in different directions it was like gazing upon different worlds. It seemed he had created a nexus in the multi-verse. He did not know how long he had been there when he heard a rustling from the nearby doorway into the partial keep.

*   *   *   *   *

L'Akyra had to make a quick get-away and slipped into her thieves' den, a dimensional pocket she had used many times to escape getting caught by danger. Sticky fingers, light steps and disappearing in the shadows were crafts of her trade and silent death was her twin. She was a high member, at least in a way, of a secret society that specialized in such things. It had benefits, wealth, prestige, and rewards you might not see otherwise, but it was dangerous too, always making you the target of others who may not even know who you are.

There was an odd glow, something was wrong with her thieves' den. She turned around quickly, where was she? She was in her den, but there was an open door and window letting light through, that seemed out of place. She backed out through the door and found herself in a garden she had never seen before that was not there from the other side before passing through the door. She regained her balance quickly; experience has advantages too.

He sat like a statue in the garden and watched her back through the door with a confused look on her face. Her green eyes almost glowed; her red fiery locks were enveloped in an aurora as they were hit by the sun. Her outfit was exotic against her shifting skin color. There were layers to this woman, his knowledge as an Ancient let him know things. It seemed she appeared different at different times. She heard his breath and turned looking straight at him almost releasing a throwing dagger that had appeared out of nowhere, before realizing he was not threatening.

"This is wrong." she whispered, more to herself then to him. "Who are you and how do you come to be here?" Her voice was melodic, enticing, but concise and articulate at the same time.

"I could ask the same of you." he stated in a deliberately calming tone. "Your charm magic does not work on me." He pulled off his visor and smiled warmly.

She moved like a cat stalking him, circling around him at a careful distance, "very wrong" she whispered.

"This is not your thieves' den. This is the fountain gardens in the courtyard of ShadowKeep. Somehow you have opened a door from your thieves' den to my private sanctuary."

She circled around coming back into his range of vision, her eyes getting caught in his. Something touched inside of both of them, but neither reacted. "How do you know of a thieves' den?" feigning no knowledge of what he was talking about.

"I am HonorLord, High Lord of ShadowKeep. There is much I know from listening to the winds of knowledge." He pulled the knowledge of situations and events through his abilities as an Ancient but was not ready to reveal this to her. "I will do you no harm, you can put your weapon up or not, it is up to you." He watched as she stopped directly in front of him about two arms lengths away.

She flipped her dagger, caught it, making it suddenly vanish into thin air. He could hear her heart beat heavy even as his own. She seemed to hear his also. "I am L'Akyra. Did you bring me here?"

"I do not know milady, I don't think so, but it is still my pleasure to meet you." he took a deep breath. He wanted her, it was not the magic and it was not her looks although he found her to be possibly one of the most attractive woman his eyes had beheld. Something inside him told him they were meant to be together. He became overly conscious of his sword 'SoulReaper' hanging at his side, "If I did, it was accidentally, this was a pocket between dimensions."

"My lord." neither had moved, but the distance between them was gone and their lips touched in a soft kiss and for a moment he felt weightless. One word slipped through his thoughts *Stralina* and they pulled apart.

"Hello, milady." he whispered unable to keep the passion completely out of his voice.

"Hello, my lord." she responded, her voice echoing his passion. Could this still be her thieves' den, he said 'was' past tense, meaning it had been changed, "Was? What have you done?" He was a strong experienced warrior, one of authority and power, perhaps there was wealth here she could harvest, perhaps an alliance she could use. The society does not need to know of this until she learns more for herself. He smells good too. Her displacer beast was still hidden in the corner where they entered the garden. He may not even know she has back up, but she decided not to tempt the situation.

"This is a copy of the garden at Shadow Keep." The kindness of his soul touched her from his voice. "Perhaps you did something that brought you here at the same time."

She paused; *something she did might have brought her here? Slipping into her thieves' den?* Was this the hand of the fates? Could this be the work of the being that gifted her the thieves den? "Would this place have eliminated something that was here before? I did nothing I have not done before, but this is not my, .. um the place I normally go." *'Careful what you say'* she thought to herself.

He knew some of what she was keeping but did not want to pry into her secrets. "Well, I don't need to know what you were doing or why or anything like that. If though you were doing something that carried you through a dimensional shift, the ripple of change may have brought you here." He looked in her eyes again as she stood in front of him. "I can get you back to wherever you came from or where you were going." He kissed her again.

She let herself slip into the sweet softness of his kiss, so powerful and tender at the same time. His hand caressed her side, and she was very aware of his wrist sliding up from her waist. She reached towards his waist and her fingers brushed the hilt of his sword. Her shudder broke their kiss.

"That blade drinks souls, too many already in my hand. You do not want to touch it if you do not need to." He unfastened the belt and stood the blade against a stone statue and with her hand pulled L'Akyra to a bench by the fountain in the middle of the garden.

She had seen this type of sword before, but could not describe if she wanted to, what she felt and heard when her fingers touched it. "I have seen blades of such making before." she said in a cavalier tone. She did not know why she spouted the words without thinking. She gave herself to his kiss. She reached for the fastenings on his chest as she felt her own garments slipping open.

The only thing left in his mind now was her as they both gave themselves over to the passion of destiny that felt as if it had always been there and brought them together as one. Their garments and belongings fell to the ground in disarray. This was the first time that they had ever met, but it felt like they had been together forever. Both L'Akyra and HonorLord were lost to the giving in to the greater passion of the moment, the force that drove them. Their bodies entwined as they stretched out on their sides on the stone bench by the fountain the cool mist enhancing and contrasting the warmth of their skin touching.

His fingers and lips danced on her skin like magic causing her desires to boil within. She closed her eyes and bathed in the fires he stirred, gave herself to his sweet fondling, where it drove the fires of her soul. Her own fingers roaming fondling, her lips caressing and dancing over his skin exploring as much of him as she could. Their bodies driving together like ocean waves beating on the shore in a rhythmic natural flow. Time was lost and the frenzy they summoned in each other kept rising.

They rolled from the bench into the cool water of the fountain, but other than brief laughter it did not slow down the rising tides of desire and passion rushing between them turning to a primal force. They lost themselves to passion fierce and uncontrolled. The sounds of pleasure they shared would have drawn much attention had they not been secluded in a private garden between dimensions. Their souls blended as one with the shuddering in release given over completely to each other, rhythms slowed, and passion softened.

Vision cleared as they gazed into each other's eyes, still entwined, embracing and bodies as one in the water. They stared into each other's eyes, just holding one another and saying nothing. Passion was shared through every pore in their bodies and neither of them wanted to let the feelings pass. Their lips touched, gentle soft nibbling kisses, fingers traveling in tender caresses with gentle loving passion. Every breath hot, their souls locked in tender bonding, he felt her wave of heat pass over him again, eyes locked deep in his. She smiled warmly with satisfaction when she felt his warmth fill the depths of her soul. Their eyes locked still lost in the windows of the others soul.

Eventually they emerged from the fountain and sat again upon the bench letting the warm air lift the moisture from their skin. They took the time to admire each other, letting time slip by with the soft touches of passing passion.

"My lady, I would that we could hold this time forever."

"My lord, you have taken captive my passion in such a way I cannot understand."

"My Lady you restore the life in my soul,

You fill the gaps and make me whole,

Your smile lifts all troubles away,

That with you I would forever stay."

She smiled at his words, "You are noble and a poet." she kissed his lips.

"This tryst I sense shall not be our only, nor I sense shall either of us forget when it passes to the next."

*   *   *   *   *

Gaharias searched the parts of the world that were assigned to him. He used his powers of divination to look everywhere. He had the creatures of the land search for him. He even used the trick they had recently learned from ShadowDancer and generated multiples of his own form to search with his own eyes. He chuckled at that too, millennium pass for him and he learns how to be a better ancient from a child.

While he did not find Jaharadan, he did identify and catalog all the threats that seemed to be linked to the changing events. Gaharias was more mature than he used to be, but he could still taste some of the thrill they used to have. The Ancients used to make games of pitting their people against each other testing their skill and the skill of their peoples. The elves were the first peace makers and oddly the humans that came from earth also tried to make peace. Somewhere along the way the Ancients started to realize the races of people they had placed on Ethar were more than just toys in a sandbox for them to play with.

Gaharias went to speak with Arimith Barhallah, high priest of the Uklian elves. Arimith was in the temple, in the seat of life facing the alter, reading through an old book of healing.

"Greetings Arimith." Gaharias spoke from the statue on the alter in front of him.

Arimith carefully laid a green woven ribbon between the pages he was reading before closing the book and setting it to the side. He lifted his eyes, keeping his head bowed slightly, "Greetings, my lord Gaharias. I am honored that you have offered your voice to my ear."

Gaharias stepped from the statue. "Your greeting is gracious and without shadow of trouble. Yet there is trouble that I would not have you in the dark concerning." A chair appeared as Gaharias sat down by the altar, beckoning Arimith to sit.

Arimith stood with respect as Gaharais appeared and sat as indicated. "I trust to your wisdom and guidance, as do the rest of our people."

"There is an evil shadow of the past that has awakened as you are aware. You may have read about Jaharadan, perhaps in history documents."

"That seems a less significant name from when the Dark Council went their own way."

"Tell the Elkinshane I want scouts to fan out and watch deeper into the territory outside of the Uklian. He needs to be prepared to send aid to the other races should they need it. The Southlands marched north and saved the Uklian previously, it is a debt that we may yet repay."

"You have given more strength to the Adoma again my lord; perhaps you want us to expand the reach of the Uklian? There are still unclaimed lands outside our boundaries."

"That may not be a bad idea at a later time, but for now I have increased the strength for your defense against what comes. You have served me well Arimith as did your ancestors. It is time I grant you the full powers of an avatar. I grant you an extent of my own power." Placing a hand on Arimith's shoulder and power surged through the High Priest, "You are numbered a little lower than the Ancients. Use the power you have been given with humility."

*   *   *   *   *

Jahaln ghost stepped from the training fields back to the entrance of the sepulcher. Aranise was there as high priestess rewarding those who willingly served Jaharadan. She bowed dutifully as Jahaln walked by, concealing the bitterness she felt for his being chosen over her. It was by her own actions she was not his equal. He ignored her as he walked on into the cool chamber.

"We have not been found yet, my young apprentice, but it will not be long till they look here." Jaharadan spread world maps over the top of one of the stone sarcophagi in the chamber. "We need to prove ourselves and make our mark so we can get recognition among the ancients. The Uklian to the west is the most powerful and experienced people of the Ancient Gaharias. To the south east are the main dwarf homelands. They too are long established and experienced under the guidance and protection of the Ancient Trelldin."

"We have number and some element of surprise on our side, lord Jaharadan." Looking at the maps. "What about the south west?"

"A young kingdom protected by new Ancients, proof that others can still get exalted to Ancient status. We might be able to take advantage of their lack of experience, but they seem to be in alliance with the elves and the dwarfs."

"We have the Milmorg, the Prak, the Nobs and the wonks will be ours shortly. Half this continent will be yours, isn't that enough to demand recognition? You have already claimed the peoples Darval abandoned on every continent."

"We need to impress that we can challenge another Ancient as they did in old in a display of conquest and power. Then we can demand our status and they will have to listen." Jaharadan pointed lower on the map. "Here is where we will make out move. The middle continents have only one inexperienced new Ancient who has made no display of power. The peoples there are not all united, they still have their scattered kingdoms."

"It seems a large number of the Ancients have abandoned Ethar. That does appear to be a rather easy target. It will take time to portal our forces there."

"We have time. We will keep the Milmorgs here, they will be our people when we are done." Jaharadan examined the map a little longer. "That settles it, we will take the middle continent and challenge this new ancient. We should probably try to find out the name of our adversary."

Jahaln interlocked his fingers and rubbed his thumbs together in thought. "We know a little about him. This ancient of the middle continent is not well known and has few followers if any. There have not been any reports of great feats that he has performed to earn his place as an ancient. How do we know he is there?"

"I can feel the presence of his influence. He is more subtle than most. Surely his hiding shows his weakness. His center of influence appears to be within Shadow Keep. That is a small Keep in the side of a mountain protecting a small village. That will be the focused goal of all our invading forces. We will bring the daemons from the forbidden continent in from the east coast, our skeletal armies will march down from the northern valleys along with the armies we gather from the northern continent. And we have gained enough influence in the southern kingdoms of the middle continent to turn their greed and lust into our allies." Jaharadan pointed to the map as he described each action.

"We have other peoples under our influence on every continent; don't we want to focus it all on the victory?" Jahaln inquired.

Jaharadan let out a dark laugh, "They are there to stir trouble and keep the attentions of the other ancients so that they do not decide to come to the aid of the real battle. Our numbers are already superior to those we wish to depose."

"I bow to your wisdom."

"Draft battle plans for invading every continent and leave copies of them all in the tombs to be found after we are gone."

Jahaln nodded, "And leave more reason for everyone to hold back and defend their own lands."

*　　*　　*　　*　　*

Merlin gathered the few items he needed for his journey, they did not have the influence here they had long ago on earth, but they had the freedom to do as they chose. He would take a boat from Dragoncove and slip out into the mist and darkness of the night when he got there. For now, he needed to travel fast.

"My Lord Talmorg, I must be going now. I will return as soon as I can, though I do not know how long I will be away."

"Merlin, you have always been a loyal friend of the kingdom, you will be welcome back. As much as I would stop you from leaving, I will not begrudge you your freedom. I am sure what you do must be important for you to leave at a time like this."   Talmorg had already offered Merlin access to anything he might need for his journey and he and Saphrine were busy dealing with the affairs of the kingdom and could not spare the time for long good-byes.

Merlin slipped out through the crowd in the room and then in through the castle to his room. Looking around, Merlin caste a light enchantment that would let him know if anything was disturbed while he was away. He stepped out on to the balcony and lifted his walking staff. With a few words, he worked the spell he had learned from Hesheil and walked the beam of light to the docks of Dragoncove. Nobody seemed to notice as he virtually appeared on the less used dock where there were several row boats moored.

He slipped down into the nearest boat and sat down. Light walking always made him hungry, so he pulled the bundle he prepared for this purpose out and calmly ate the chunk of bread and cheese as he looked around at the port. There seemed to be more activity than he recalled and a sense of urgency. Word had reached them that something was amiss, although there really was not more than rumors of what it might be. He finished off the last morsels of his food and carefully folded the cloth it had been bundled in and returned it to his bag.

Moving to the front of the boat to undo the lashings holding it to the dock, Merlin heard a sword slide through the hasp of a scabbard. "Stop, who are you, old man stealing away in the shadows and attempting to off with a boat?"

Turning and deliberately righting himself, "This is my boat." His eyes met with the guard's eyes, "Gerralic, why do you delay me in my business." He smiled almost laughing and extended a hand of friendship.

"Merlin?" The man paused and put up his sword. "Forgive me old friend, things have gotten a little tense around here and mischief always follows. Come share a drink and a story or two before you slip off again." They shook hands.

"My friend, this time I cannot, but I promise when the storm passes, I shall return, and we shall drink and tell stories till the lanterns burn out in the Inn." Merlin looked out into the fog that hid the waters of the cove. "And no, I cannot tell you what I am up to nor take you with me. Perhaps when I return, I will be able to tell you more."

"As you wish, then I shall tell no one of your passing." Gerralic helped him with the ropes and pushed him off into the waters.

He could feel the direction as he paddled steadily out into the water. The mist enveloped him, and the world vanished. All that was left for his eyes was the boat that carried him. He reached the point and stopped. Standing in the boat he drew on the power of the goddess and parted the fog. An island appeared in front of him, protected by sea serpents that parted to allow him passage.

Merlin rowed the rest of the way to shore and tied the boat to a bush near the water. Up the path from the beach were two young women dressed in robes, in service to the goddess Bridgit Ceridwen. Merlin gathered his belongings from the boat and walked up to meet them.

"Welcome to Avalon, Merlin." They spoke in unison. "The Lady of the Depths awaits you. She foresaw your arrival."

Merlin noted that he had been gone long enough that the younger priestesses did not know him. "Most gracious of you to offer escort."

Merlin knew this place, but they lead the way giggling and watching him like a novelty. He could see the great tree in the middle of the island over the rooftops as they approached the main manor house. As they walked in the front door, he breath in the earthen scents that filled the air. "My Brigit Ceridwen, I have been away too long."

"Indeed, you have." The Lady of the Depths stepped in from a door across the room from him. The high priestess of Brigit always surrendered her name to her title, but Merlin knew who she used to be also.

"Well, I will always serve the goddess as long as she will have me do so." Merlin gave a somewhat awkward bow leaning on his staff making it a bit lopsided.

"And you serve the goddess giving your wisdom and knowledge to those who serve Ancients on Ethar? Do you not wish to reclaim the old world on earth?" The Lady baited him.

"I will serve Brigit wherever she whims I should be. The Ancients of this world welcome her as one of their own if she wishes it." He sat in an overstuffed chair to the side of the room and relaxed into it. "As I recall, earth seems to have turned a blind back to all the gods of old."

"And they would lock up the likes of you where you could not reach out to the world around." She sat a more formal chair with a high back near him. "Merlin my friend, I have been expecting you and the answers are:" Her eyes traveled to the vision as it came over her. "He will achieve his goal, but not what he wants. Old powers here are stepping aside for new and step up to do more. The goddess will make sure her loyal followers will have a place although it is no place."

Merlin sat alert as she spoke. "Three unasked questions and three unresolved answers. Gracious still is her favor."

"You really should be less shaded in your devotion." The Lady of the Depths laughed, "You have her favor. East of Tolgus Ridge and North West of the Endless Caves is the Crypt where Jaharadan slept all these years. He will be departed from there before anyone can reach him. He has no real plans of attacking anywhere on the northern continent."

"That is good news. That also means that we have no immediate interest in Jaharadan other than keep good relations with the Ancients."

"One more thing," the Lady looked at Merlin speculatively, "the goddess wishes you to bring her ten loyal followers from this land that will give themselves totally to her. For this favor, she will elevate your powers and release your oath, that you may freely serve her as you will."

"I am honored. I serve by choice now; the oath is but decoration on my dedication." Merlin rubbed his chin in thought, "There are easily ten in Dragoncove, but I will look elsewhere also."

The Lady waved her hand over the basin of mercury on the small table between them. A great army appeared, marching through a wide forested valley. At closer examination, it was an army of skeletons. A shiny shadow flashed through the ranks leaving debris of bones and armor behind. The scene changed to daemons and vampire creatures flying to a beach from boats on an ocean. Then to gargoyles and various beast races lumbering through forested hills. Then the images in the mercury faded.

"You will travel to the middle continent, but you will spend two days here first." She stood up and beckoned him to follow.

CHAPTER 6

One Domino

Chareece took the opportunity to return to her father's home as soon as she was back in her room. She split between Chareece and ShadowDancer and as ShadowDancer she returned to the strange house in the strange world from whence her father came. It seemed appropriate to her that since as ShadowDancer she was the daughter of the ancient Eric, that was the form she should use to visit his home. She found herself again in the same place she was before. She turned to her left and stepped into the area that had what looked like a stone floor and started looking around, she had to be careful, she knew nothing about this world.

Judging by the dishes and pots and pans in this room, she guessed it was a kitchen of sorts. Devices with knobs and buttons, ShadowDancer was glad she was familiar with the Eftites or she would have recognized much less of what was here then she did. She thought twice about trying to turn anything or push buttons, not knowing what they might do, this could be some kind of laboratory too. She heard a bell go off in the house and then a noise from the door the other side of what looked like a dining area or perhaps study area, quickly she vanished into the shadows.

A human much older looking stepped in and dropped something she pulled out of the door in her pocket, ShadowDancer guessed it was a key of some sort. ShadowDancer slipped through the shadows and out the door to avoid getting caught in this house by the stranger who had just entered. She just wanted to explore her father's world a little, not start trouble.

The grass outside the house was not naturally grown to look the way it did, it had been cut and gave the appearance of an even length. Strange walkways surrounded the small patterns of grass and other plants were placed by design giving them also an unnatural look while still holding an appeal to the eye. There was a large carriage in a wider flat stone area that lead down to the street. The street itself was also covered in an unfamiliar material. A carriage similar to the one in the yard moved past without horses, much like a machine Shiheel had built. The man riding in the carriage seemed to be controlling the movement. There was much to see, so much to explore, she was not certain which way to go so she started following the roads, slipping unseen through the shadows.

ShadowDancer followed the movement of the carriages in the directions that they appeared to get denser. She came to a bridge that spanned a river and chose to travel in the shadows under the bridge, examining the structure with intrigue as she passed to the other side. She wondered for a moment if this bridge of stone and metal could withstand the heat of the chasm of lava. There were three people under the bridge gathered around a small fire wearing rather threadbare clothing. She stopped and listened to their conversation. Their language was similar to the common language of the humans back home. They had a strange accent and dialect making it difficult for her to clearly follow everything they said, at the same time very similar to the way her father Eric spoke at times. What she did pick up from their conversation seemed to be they needed food and were going to have to find shelter somewhere if it got any colder.

They were not totally unlike some of the outcasts she had helped before. Moving just out of their line of sight she stepped out of the shadows and walked back over to where they were seated. The first to see her was the man in the middle and he said gruffly in her direction, "We are not bothering anyone, leave us to our business." The others turned and looked at her.

"I am a friend." she stated in as calming a voice as she could.

"She's naked." the man on the right said to his companions in a low whisper.

"You won't find any business down here." the lady on the left piped in, "We ain't got no money."

The exact meaning of the second statement the lady made was not clear to ShadowDancer other than the no money. She gestured and a low table with cushions appeared with a small feast laid out upon it appeared in front of them. "Sit and eat friends." They stared at her and the table a bit dumbfounded, she found herself taking their hands and coaxing them to be seated and enjoy a meal.

The one man pinched the other on the arm and asked, "Are we dreaming?"

"That don't feel like no dream to me." the other snipped, yanking his arm away from the pinch.

The lady was stuffing food from the table into her bag and pockets, taking a bite out of a piece here and there. ShadowDancer had set an enchantment to heal their minor illnesses and injuries as they ate and watch their postures improve as they felt more comfortable.

"Does this land take gold and silver coin for exchange?" ShadowDancer asked wanting to assist them further with their needs.

"What land doesn't" The man looked up from where he was eating between the other two. "I am Jack, this is Danny and Steph" he stated pointing to the others with the drumstick he was eating. "Who are you?"

She caught herself before she gave her name, "I am known as ShadowDancer."

"Are you a demon or an angel?" Stephanie asked.

"I am neither, just a visitor offering help as I pass through." with another gesture a small pouch appeared next to each of them containing a handful of gold and silver coins, and with another gesture a stack of clothing appeared by each also, although the clothing was formal wear that she was familiar with and she did not know how it would compare to the clothing in this world yet. "This should help you get back on your feet, I must keep moving. I would only ask what I ask of all my people, that you help others."

She spent a few days wandering helping those in need that she stumbled across and learning what she could about this strange world. She spent the greater part of a day with a young street girl who taught her how to blend in and how to dress. She knew time was not tracking the same for her as Chareece as it was for her as ShadowDancer. She pulled herself back together as Chareece in her room. Her world needed her right now, she could try learning about her heritage and her father's world another time. Less than five minutes had passed for Chareece. She decided she would deal with the time anomaly and any further attempts to learn about her father's world at a later time when there was not a war to worry about. She stood up and set her mind on the matters at hand.

Chareece was becoming very comfortable being in two or three places at a time. Occasionally she was in even more locations especially when she was conversing with Melina and Jeyra. They embraced serving her and she talked to them frequently in her private rooms. Gaharias explained to her that these rooms she was building were not in her mind, but she was actually building an existence, much like a dimension of her own. She was not fully clear on what he was explaining, but she understood she was creating it and it was actually a real place separate from Ethar.

Melina and Jeyra, both now as her servants, took on being clothed in fire and shadow. As much as she tried to stop the rituals before they made it to a sacrifice, she had already spared several others from the soul stealer daggers. ShadowDancer expanded her realm to accommodate those who chose to stay with her. She used her home palace as a guide forming the inner court and outer court, surrounded by the Royal gardens and then the residential chambers. This gave them space and comfort for now.

Melina was placed in authority, and Jeyra had free run of things also. Jeyra was not committed to staying once things on Ethar had been settled, but she was considering the matter. The others were all happy to be there in service to ShadowDancer having chosen to be there. There were a couple that chose not to join ShadowDancer but be released to move on. She summoned Jeyra and Melina to the inner court.

"Jeyra, you know your homelands and while you cannot interact with your people, you can travel with a thought from place to place. I want you to move between the sacrificial alters they have set up and alert me when they show signs of having a gathering." ShadowDancer instructed her in the privacy of the chambers she had created for them.

"I shall do as you will, Milady." Jeyra kept her eyes on ShadowDancer expectantly.

Shadow Dancer, paused a slight moment, "With my blessings be on your way, child." Jeyra vanished with a thought.

"Melina, your sister and her followers know what they are looking for. Have her instruct them to fan out throughout the lands and alert us if they see signs of followers of Jaharadan anywhere else in the southlands."

"Milady," She smiled with excited pleasure, "it is my honor to serve." Melina gave a very flourished courtesy.

Shadow Dancer felt honored, "Quickly to your sister now. Tell her they need not carry a burden as they travel. The land will yield her bounty for my people." She said warmly, not fully realizing the extent of the boon she just gifted to her followers.

As Melina vanished, so also did this iteration of ShadowDancer.

*   *   *   *   *

ShadowDancer had scoured the south lands and north along the borders of both her family ruled side and that with fealty to the dwarf kingdom. The threats were not there. As she moved north, she found that the peoples under the influence of Jaharadan seemed to be moving away from the powerful established kingdoms on the continent. She pulled back to Chareece.

Chareece went out to Talmorg and Saphrine, instead of sending a handmaiden this time. They had already sent half of their armies to the northern borders to be ready for any attack. Half of the remaining forces were patrolling the kingdom and still assisting the people in recovering from the tremendous destruction of the cracking of the world. The throne room as not as busy as it had been, but there was still a steady flow of activity.

"Father."

Talmorg looked up, "Yes Chareece?"

"They are not coming to attack any of the established kingdoms on this continent. They seem to be getting ready to go elsewhere, although I have not been able to determine where they will attack, yet." She had a pensive thoughtful look on her face.

"Why do think this, dear?" Talmorg slipped into the familiar seeing the intensity of his daughter's expression. "How will they move armies from here to somewhere else to go to war?"

Saphrine stepped up, "They are led by a necromancer, those arts have ways of stepping through the realms of the dead to travel to other places. We should alert the religious orders to be alert for any activity in the realms of the dead."

"He is not trying to conquer the world he is after a display of power. He wants recognition. He is going to go," She broke off her sentence. "We are prepared, but I think we are safe from harm." ShadowDancer was headed to the middle continents, Hans needed to know what she knew. Another iteration of Shadow Dancer appeared near an altar where Jeyra called her, to break the spell over another group of followers. Hopefully this time without a sacrifice happening. Melina was reporting there were no further signs of the dark cult followers in the southland kingdoms, but they were still looking.

"We cannot get help to Hans in time without help." Saphrine stated with a sigh. "We have been distracted so as to be unable to lend aid in the real battle."

"Indeed, our troops are already spread throughout the kingdom, and even if they were back it would take days of preparation and means faster than by boat to get there." Talmorg added.

"I am going to take my leave. I will find a way to help, but I will need to focus my power to be of real value." Chareece spoke softly and the three of them moved to one of the chambers out of sight and earshot of others.

"What do you mean, dear?" Saphrine asked. Talmorg had an expression indicating he already suspected something.

"You have heard of Shadow Dancer, haven't you?"

They both half-nodded at her question. Saphrine whispered "There are rumors of a new young goddess who cares for the less favored." Her eyes widened a little.

"I am her." Chareece changed in front of her parents

"I was right in not questioning your night activity anymore." Talmorg nodded, then uncertain how to act in her presence as one of the ancients he half bowed and hesitated to look at her seeing still his daughter dressed in flames and flame like shadows.

"Don't treat me different, you still raised me. You are my parents."

"Do you have to run around naked though?" Saphrine asked almost in tears and not sure why.

"Oh, mom, nothing is showing, I am dressed in fire and shadow, that is all, modesty is preserved. When I first started realizing my power, I did not know how to make my clothing vanish so I could move unseen." She blushed and paused a moment. "Then while I was out there, I stumbled across someone in trouble. I saw how a torch was lit and the fire hid the burning torch beneath it. Acting quickly, I used that to conceal my nakedness, when I appeared and warded off the young lady's attackers."

"How did you know you could help?" Talmorg asked.

"Honestly, at first, I didn't know, but I started discovering many things I could do. I kept them hidden because I did not want to worry you. This though is big, and I am already a part of it, so I think it is best you know who I am."

Saphrine stumbled over words. "Why didn't you change the way you appear after the first time? You didn't have to keep this look and if you have learned to make your clothing vanish with you now, you could appear as yourself."

"The description spread quickly and those who called upon my help expected me to look like this. It also conceals who I am so that I would not be identified as Princess Chareece. This way I can keep my identity as princess separate from Shadow Dancer the goddess or ancient." She reached over and hugged her mom. "You are still my mom, that will never change." she pulled Talmorg into the embrace, "And you will always be my dad, even as Eric is my father."

"I trust you will be well." Talmorg maintained his control. "We will be anxious for your return."

*　　*　　*　　*　　*

Eric and Bonny had arrived in Dragoncove to find defenses were on full alert, but no threat was to be found. They too discovered that those who may have posed a threat seemed to be vanishing to the north, and even vanishing all together. They met with the Council and military high command in the city council building.

"It is better to be ready when the time is ripe and have no enemy, then not to heed warning and be taken unprepared." High Commander Keltirous McLodden stated.

Eric nodded, "Indeed, but if they are not waging war with their armies anywhere on the northern continent, where are they sending them?"

"Rumors from the port indicate there are weird armies and cults springing up everywhere and trouble for the middle continents. Those are rumors and cannot be counted on for any fact." Councilman Drek Cierden commented.

"Hans!" Bonny looked concerned. "I don't think he can be defeated, but he may need our help."

"He has not called for us, perhaps we are all chasing ghosts and there is no real immediate threat. The 'would be threat' seems to have moved north into the mountains, perhaps we should pursue them and see if we can stop them before trouble starts. Then we can go from there to ShadowKeep." Eric looked speculative, "This way we can be sure the threat is gone from here and help there if needed."

Everyone seemed to like this plan except for Bonny, but she too saw reasonable thought and conceded to taking Eric's approach. Eric Paused, "The magic races all have a connection with the land through the adomas created by their ancients at the centers of their civilizations. The time will come soon when Dragoncove shall gain a bond with the land."

*　　*　　*　　*　　*

Darval called to Gaharias from the northern mountains overlooking the ocean on the middle continent. "I have slipped through all the residual peoples I have on Ethar. They have prospered more than I expected. Now Jaharadan has taken control of all of them."

"As we suspected he would try, thinking you are no longer here to care." Gaharias stated. "Not exactly something out of line or character with a remnant of the dark councils power."

"This is true, but it was by heavy-handed methods I gained controlling influence over the dark council." Darval shook his head. "Not to be distracted, Jaharadan has his focus on taking this continent entirely and his armies are almost in place. My remnant of people turned into his armies."

"We do not have time to match forces." Gaharias observed.

"AND I don't want to. I have been working on taking control of my people away from Jaharadan and his followers. The chemists in the City of Talmorg indicate they are close to a counter agent for the controlling toxins in the blood samples, but my daemons and vampires may have the ability to override the influence themselves given time."

"The quake eliminated the leadership at ShadowKeep with the exception of Hans Spardic and he was not there when it hit. Perhaps it was more of an attack then we calculated."

"If he is successful or even close to proving he can be a challenger, he will be claiming he has rights to recognition as an Ancient." Darval pulled his eyes away from the ocean and looked at Gaharias. "The dark elves from the shadow realms are in ShadowKeep ready to assist in the defense. I have asked Hans to attempt to avoid direct combat with the living races, especially those coming in by ship to give me time to attempt to remove the cursed control."

"I have a few loyal still in the village of Shadow Keep. I can grant them the powers of avatars to aid in the fight. I am sure I have pushed the limits of the accord, but I am not going to turn my back." Gaharias shook his head, "There are times I regret signing that agreement."

"It has saved Ethar from destruction, brother and our children are no longer dieing in battle against each other." Darval laughed, "The dark council has changed so much having room and free reign of their own races. They have actually become more civilized only having each other to fight against. Destruction somehow lost its savor with nobody building anything good to destroy. With peace, the members of the dark council have started recognizing their people have more virtue than just pieces in a game."

"So, what are the forces closing in on ShadowKeep?"

"Lord Valdir and Balgrin are coming in by ship they have already started landing on the eastern coast. Necromancers running armies of skeletons and risen dead have started forming in the northern coastal end of the valley that sweeps down through the middle of the continent. The daemons and bestial armies of the western continent have crossed over and are climbing the mountains from the western coast. The southern kingdoms of the middle continent have sworn allegiance with Jaharadan for the promise of possession of ShadowKeep."

"They have the numbers; this does not look good."

"On the good side, the Barony of Pendril has uprooted and moved into ShadowKeep submitting themselves to Hans as the new High Lord of ShadowKeep. The scattered baronies and free realms will also gather to the defense of the last vestige of freedom."

"We should head there and see what we can do to help." Gaharias stated and stepped with Darval to their destination.

*   *   *   *   *

Vorka and Arco were welcomed when they reached the Walled City of Talmorg. They were treated as honored guests and given a place to stay as ambassadors in the palace. They were not used to being treated with this much honor; they had not been intended as the official representatives. Now they found themselves seated with Talmorg and Saphrine at a meal in their honor. There was time between events waiting for news.

"So, the proposal you bring is open trade." Talmorg stated over the feast. "I think that is a great idea and should bring our people closer again. We will find a way to cross that great gap once we are free of the current crisis."

"I no have the documents." Arco stated. "sorry bout that. I was not the supposed to be bearer."

"That is not a problem." Saphrine stated graciously, "Perhaps when things have settled, we can meet face to face with your king to accept initial proposals and discuss future option."

"Yeah." Arco answered, not exactly what you would expect from a diplomat, but then again, they were not exactly the diplomats of their original party. They did however lay the groundwork for the trade agreement that would later unite all of the southlands.

*   *   *   *   *

Racken was a little disappointed that the Kingdom of Talmorg was not able to do much for his people. He knew they had their best minds working on something that would counter the dark magics that controlled his people, but then he was not sure what it was he expected. He sat in his lavish room in the palace searching his mind for anything else he might do to help his people.

"Don't be afraid." The Lady spoke stepping in from his balcony.

He turned and recognized her immediately, "Shadow Dancer." He stood up and bowed deep in flourished respect.

"You worry for your people. There is little that can be done by others, but for your comfort I tell you what is being done."

"Even if they succeed in the cure for the disease that controls them, it will be too late to deliver it."

"At the rate I am going with Jeyra, we may have all of your peoples freed before the cure is found."

"Jeyra? Who is that?" Racken looked confused

"Um, she is dead. She is a heroine to your people, because she is watching the altars of Jaharadan and helping to stop the blood sacrifices that are holding the control over your people." The young Milmorg girl appeared before Racken. As a vision and then vanished.

Hope filled his eyes, "I am honored to have met you. If Darval should not choose to return to us, I will turn to you, ShadowDancer."

CHAPTER 7

Preparation

HonorLord returned to ShadowKeep his mind was more focused. He still felt the loss of his wife and the ache was still there, but he was able to keep his mind on the matters at hand. Repairs were sufficient that there were again only two ways into ShadowKeep, up the precipice trail to the front gates or fly in over the mountain rim. He would prefer to keep the battle away from the keep and the village if possible and with the help of the dark elves from the shadow realms a plan was forming.

With the commanding ranks of the armies of the dark elves, Pendril and ShadowKeep he worked over maps and laid out strategies. Proposals were made, counter proposals and adjustments. Hans used everything he knew to update and keep the information on the tables accurate.

"The numbers are great," he continued, "but their movement and skill is diminished because they are not in control of their own actions. This goes for the armies of Deamorg coming in from the Eastern coast, the bestial armies coming in from the continents to the West and even the necromancer army of skeletons coming down the Valley from the north."

"The kingdoms to the south are coming of their own decision." Lord Rolland stated, "They have no loyalty, and the promise of granting them ShadowKeep won their favor."

"But your riders can strike at them as they travel and slow their movement without suffering too many casualties." They all looked at HonorLord as he spoke, "The loyalties of their troops are not any better than the loyalties of their leadership, morale will drop and so will their number."

"Indeed, we have done battle with them before." Lord Rolland agreed, "We may be able to diminish their number sufficiently to keep them from reaching our doorsteps."

"Every man, woman and child of able age has been equipped with enhanced weapons." Raishek, one of the Eftites that had arrived to help with the recovery from the quake. The storerooms of old weapons and armor have also been brought up to quality levels."

"Provisions have been secured and distributed to keep up the strength of our armies as they travel." Harold the chief provisioner of ShadowKeep added "We have additional supplies to support any who come to join us in our cause."

The people did not know that their newly appointed leader was the Ancient of war, so Hans was silent about the boons he had been granting worthy members of their forces. The time would come when he no longer be able to conceal that he was an Ancient from others, but for now it remained a secret.

*   *   *   *   *

ShadowDancer already had followers in the middle continents. The populations of the scattered baronies around the continent that was the home of ShadowKeep were mostly human but others who had been oppressed in their prior homelands had traveled here for the promise of freedom to run their own lives. She did not help them so they would follower her or look to her, but they did because she had helped them in times of need. She now whispered in their ears and let them know what was coming.

She did not tell them what to do. Some headed to ShadowKeep for sanctuary or to help defend their land. Others chose to take their chances, or hide, or find ways away from the paths of danger. ShadowDancer headed to ShadowKeep to do what she could to come to the aid of the defenders of this sanctuary.

*   *   *   *   *

Merlin did not head straight to ShadowKeep, he also traveled to the independent baronies. His true loyalties were to his goddess and to the Lady of the Lake. He spoke to nobility and to peasant, letting them know what was coming planting seeds for the of influence as he has always done. He used the resources he had to make items such as a staff with an embellished power or tools for peasants that would earn favor. He also nurtured the whispering of the plants and smaller living creatures of the land. These served to provide communication between the followers of the goddess and an information net for the Lady of the Lake.

The whispers from the grass and the leaves of the forest told him the armies of the enemy had landed and were preparing to start moving. "Time is growing short." he whispered to no one in particular and headed to ShadowKeep.

*   *   *   *   *

"Our time is being wasted." Bonny was irritated.

Eric nodded, she was right, "I should have listened to you sooner."

"The people of the northern continent will let us know if there is anything we are needed for here, or if they find anything. We are more needed where we can make a difference."

"And Chareece or should I say ShadowDancer is doing more for these folks then we are now." Eric looked into Bonny's eyes, "You really are beautiful when you are angry."

Bonny tried to glare at him, but his smile melted her anger away. "Hans needs us."

"I doubt he needs us, but that is probably where we can do the most good for events at hand." He took her hand and they stepped from where they were to the courtyard in Shadowkeep.

Aranise stepped from the bushes where she was hiding and examined the ground where the strangers had vanished. She turned and headed back to the crypt, she had to tell Jaharadan what she had seen and heard.

Eric and Bonny were unaware they had been observed or just how close they had come to finding what they had been searching for. They headed towards the throne room in ShadowKeep.

*   *   *   *   *

Terriala touched the sweet pepper plant in her small garden again and watched the pepper form and grow to full maturity before her eyes, plucked it and absently dropped it in the basket with the rest. Melina had told her ShadowDancer promised the land would yield its' bounty to her followers so they could travel the lands unburdened when they did her bidding. It seemed they could all bring the bounty of what they needed to harvest with a mere touch.

Terriala wondered if this was what ShadowDancer had intended. It was wonderful, they would never go hungry or lack for need of harvest-able goods. The group she was with traveled in tents. Their talents and foraging had always been how they sustained their needs. As High Priestess she now shared in the leading of the people with Samuel. She deliberately deferred as much as she could to his authority and when possible gave him the option to bring information to their tribe that was provided to her.

He had been willing to give her leadership, but she insisted that it was the right thing to keep separation between the two forms of authority. She also pointed out that it kept them both in balance and gave them someone to consult with if they were unsure of decisions that needed to be made. This new ability they had all received from ShadowDancer was cause for her to summon Samuel to meet with her in private.

"Are you going to market?" He asked as he walked into her tent.

She looked down at the basket overflowing with peppers, "Oh, no, actually I was getting lost in thought pondering the implications of what this means."

Samuel laughed, "It means we won't run out of peppers."

"Seriously!" She insisted, "We have been given the ability to bring the bounty out from any plant we touch, producing herbs we need for healing, food, even for fiber and for wood we need for crafting."

"It is truly a big blessing she has granted us."

"I think our people should keep this a secret as best we can. This is wonderful for us, but we could experience a lot of negative consequences if it gets out." Terriala observed.

"Like what?" Samuel looked at her uncertain, "overloaded wagons? Not going hungry?"

"No, I am serious. Insincere followers who join us just in hopes of gaining this power. Others seeking us out to serve their profiteering."

"Hadn't thought about it like that. Perhaps you are right." he pondered, "Now that you have me thinking in the negative bent on the subject isn't it also possible, we will be accused of stealing if we have produce and do not have an explanation for where we gained our abundance?"

"We are already accused of that because we are different, we are half breeds, and looked down upon as impure. We could use this ability to nurture farms and help others and gain their respect without them knowing what it is we actually do. It would grant us a place in every society."

Samuel picked up a rock she had been using to hold some of her papers in place. "I have one more thing to show you. I don't think you are aware of; I have heard nobody else mention this yet." As he held the stone up a crystal formed out of the top and then the different mineral components of the rock seemed to separate forming separate nodules in his hand. "I discovered this one earlier quite by accident."

"It takes some will to bring these results, I had not tried it on rocks or non-living bounties, although that is still a bounty from the land." she paused her eyes opening slightly, "You know what this can mean?!"

"You are right we need to gather our people and let them know to stay silent about the gift we have received." Samuel started to get up.

"Wait a moment." He paused and turned and Terriala continued, "Have you experimented with this? This is like being granted a power of the ancients, it is really big."

"I am not sure what you mean by experimented I did it by accident once and now again here with you. I'll go spread the word we are having a meeting this evening."

As Samuel closed the tent flap behind him, Terriala knelt down and touched the ground in her tent. First a diamond bigger than her fist rose up from the dirt. She slipped it in her pocket to conceal it. She touched the ground again and a perfect sphere of gold about an inch in diameter rose up. "I can control the shape!" she whispered. She lifted her hand and touched the ground again and considered the hardest metal in nature and closed her eyes to focus. When she opened her eyes there was a metal dagger next to her hand in the dirt made from the metal she had once seen in the mountains. She had been told it was too hard to forge weapons from. She picked up the dagger and the orb, slipping one under her robes in her belt, and the other in her pocket. "We must keep quiet about what we can do."

*   *   *   *   *

Arco and Vorka had successfully laid the groundwork for a trade treaty between the kingdoms of Talmorg and Darkalon, so their work was done. They let Talmorg know their intent to return home and their desire to resolve their concern for the companions that left Darkalon with them to start with.

"My friends," Talmorg offered, "You are welcome to stay a few days to see if this rain passes."

"My Lord, it has been raining a lot since the cracking of the world, I do not see that changing for a time. We appreciate the offer, but we long to be home again." Arco answered.

"Perhaps you will visit again when things are not so tense." Saphrine added

"I insist then at the very least you accept an escort to help you with the crossing. The lands are not as safe as they should be with the rising threat and the aftermath of the quake." Talmorg clapped Arco on the shoulder, "At least until you have the company of your own folks again."

Arco and Vorka appreciated the offer and did not resist the generosity of the Elf-Lord. They set out with two carriages and two squads of soldiers. Arco and Vorka road in the carriages and one squad road horse back in front and the other behind. The roads were a little rough with soft spots and wash outs, so their movement was slowed, but faster and dryer for them then walking.

*   *   *   *   *

They started arriving in the throne room of ShadowKeep to offer their help and advise him of events. They did not seem to realize that as the Ancient of war he gained knowledge of the movement of armies and soldiers. As an Ancient he even found himself in the position of recognizing warriors who might be in the ranks of enemies. It seemed a little awkward to him, but he found that there were principles he could apply to balance what he did. For now, though he needed rest and wanted some time apart from things.

The constant rain did not help his attitude. The Keep was high, but the valley was experiencing some flooding that was hampering the rebuilding efforts. His mind wandered and he kept finding her way into his thoughts. He stepped out of time into the alternative fountain gardens he had formed in the rift between dimensions. It had only been a week he had wanted to see her again but was surprised to see her standing by the fountain.

L'Akyra turned and looked at him inquiring, "You summoned me? You must return me to the moment and place from whence I departed, my lord. If I am not there when they open the door for me, there may be trouble."

"We can take time here and I can have you back the moment you left." He hoped he had not offended her and smiled warmly, "Forgive me any indiscretion, I wanted to see you when I came here, I did not know my want would summon you. If you do not wish to company with me I can send you back straight away."

"Oh, my lord, I have missed you since last we parted." She was surprised at her passionate outburst. "Next time please whisper in my ear and ask before pulling me away. You are sure if I stay you can return me as promised?"

"I am certain."

"Then let us enjoy the moment." L'Akyra stepped to him and they both joined in a tender embrace. Lips met softly dancing.

"How do you have my heart, while I am yet morning the loss of my wife whom I love dearly."

She pulled back, "I should let you mourn in private."

"No." he pulled her back, "You are medicine to my soul."

HonorLord removed his full-length cloak and laid it on the red paving stones of the garden and lowered her down in his embrace. She moved to his slightest bidding anxiously. They both wanted to get lost in their shared passion and forget completely about their lives for a little while. Garments parted and were tossed without care around them. Their lips and fingers exploring, indulging in getting to know each other and learning secrets, each seeking the others pleasure.

His touch drove waves of desire and pleasure through her body. Her body quaked and shuddered her thoughts lost to the ecstasy of each moment. She burned with the desire to give as much pleasure to him as he gave her. She rippled her passion and desire against his, her lips ministered kisses to his healing soul. She used every bit of herself to bring the erupting of new life to his body as only she could.

Words of passion were whispered, hearts and souls knitted together. Their pleasures crested and fell many times, before they lay exhausted in each other's arms. "We are destined to be together." he whispered his eyes lost in hers. "You will be at my side in ShadowKeep."

"I so want that." she aspirated back, "But I have obligations and unbreakable ties in my own world. Somehow I know we shall find a way."

Sleep overtook them as they lay there with entwined wrapped now against the cool air in his cloak. How long they slept didn't matter, nor could they tell who woke first. They seemed to wake up as one with a tender kiss their bodies joining again as one in the gentle act of passion. It was an act of heart felt passion as they bonded together and lay there gazing in each other's eyes before getting up and washing in the fountains of the garden. Their separate worlds were calling to them, yet they lingered as they dressed. They shared feeling and passionate bursts smiling and admiring what they saw in the other.

"It is time, love." L'Akyra stated with a touch of remorse in her voice, "You must send me back until we can meet again."

"To the moment from which you were pulled." leaning forward he kissed her again.

L'Akyra reach up and pulled a pink ribbon from her hair and tied it around the hilt of his sword. "A token and a reminder to come for me again. You have claim to my heart, and our time is ahead of us. Now send me back until next time."

With a thought she vanished back to her world. HonorLord took a moment to pull his mind back in focus to the matters of Ethar he must attend to. For now, their rendezvous was passed, and he had the promise of what was to come to pull him forward. He stepped through back into his private chamber behind the throne in ShadowKeep. He was ready now to focus on those gathering to help him defend his home and his people.

*　　*　　*　　*　　*

There was room enough in ShadowKeep to house all that had come to help defend the the protected lands of the middle continent, but in preparation for making intercept strikes there were cities of tents outside the walls ready to start marching in three different directions. They had a day of rest before they would move out. The idea was to intercept the enemies before they reached ShadowKeep and diminish their numbers before having to face them head-to-head on the battlefield.

"We are ready." HonorLord lifted up his sword as he spoke, "For the defense of the lands and the glory of the free lands, Salarikian shall lead the command of the dark elves to the east to keep the Deamorg busy and delay them from reaching ShadowKeep. The fastest and most adept third of his forces will be traveling with him. Lord Rolland of Pendril and ShadowKeep will be leading a force West and south to intercept the armies of the southern kingdom, to use lightning strikes and vanishing to reduce their numbers and delay their arrival. I shall lead a mixed army to the west to intercept the skeletal army and the bestial army. Drakalon and a third part of the dragons defending ShadowKeep will travel with me. A third part of the great birds of the north will also travel with me. Our final fall-back point is ShadowKeep where the majority of our forces will wait ready to cover our fall back. Remember our strategies are to delay and reduce numbers in the enemy ranks. They will be war-worn before they reach ShadowKeep, if they make it this far. Darvarias will sit as temporary High-lord until my return."

Eric stepped up, "Bonny and I will assist from here, defending ShadowKeep and reaching out to answer you on the field. Do not hesitate to ask us when you need us." As Eric finished speaking, he captured the moment to respond to a request from a Uklian scout.

Eric recognized Shadoweaver. Elkeriah was his real name, Shadoweaver his title. The moment capture, the Uklian elf had dropped his guard and found himself surrounded by a mix of wonks and skeletons. He was in a tree holding them at a distance with fire blasts. Shadoweaver had found the hide-away of the liche and was carrying a bag full of battle plans. Eric pull Shadoweaver into the moment.

"So, he was holding up in the ancient burial ground of the high elves?"

Shadoweaver fumble a moment before recognizing Eric, "Yes"

Eric placed a hand on Shadoweaver's shoulder and stepped with him a couple miles closer to the Uklian forest taking him clear of the immediate danger. "So, you found invasion plans for every continent. Most of them are intended to be found to keep the world divided. The armies left behind are small and I do not think they will attack the Uklian but take what you found back to the Elkinshane."

Eric was back in the war room and released the moment, "There are contingency armies of the lich on all continents to insure they do not come to our assistance."

Merlin spoke up, "My mission is to locate the Liche, he slipped away from the northern continent just before he was discovered. The grass and the trees will not let him stay hidden again."

Others spoke out the roles they played and then the banquet was served. In the morning they would be moving out.

*   *   *   *   *

ShadowDancer stayed hidden she observed the war room at ShadowKeep and was out scouting in four directions at the same time. The other Ancients knew she was there, and she could sense each of them. There were a couple other Ancients she had not met before that seemed to be observing events, but not participating. All of the ancients knew what Ancients were there, because they could feel each other's presence.

The Deamorg army was massive on the beaches already and still pouring in from the over the water, from ships farther out then she could see from the beach. As long as she was just observing from the shadows, ShadowDancer was comfortable being in five places at once. The southern kingdom also had an army on the move, although they were barely out of the capital city and seemed to be taking a more casual march. She had the impression they were marching in hopes of getting their prize and missing the fight. They were she noted marching of their own accord, not under the mind control she had seen with the Milmorg or the Deamorg.

The bestial army was climbing the cliffs of the western coast. They seemed fierce and powerful, but not organized, occasionally swiping at each other. They did not seem to have unity or purpose, and while they seemed to be partially under the same mind control, she had seen before, they did not seem to be as controllable. It was like habits of instinct overrode the mind that was being controlled. It was the ocean of the skeletal army moving down to the lush central valley from the northern coast that caused her to gasp at its mere size. They were a threat by number even if they had not been also wearing armor and carrying weapons. In their path they left nothing alive. The ground itself seemed to die around them. ShadowDancer felt anger at this destruction of everything living.

She would search for those behind this. The lich and any who helped. She knew without having to use her Ancient ability that there were others practicing necromancy helping to make an army this large. Her anger burst a circle of flames around her, over a thousand skeletons were consumed and turned to ash. ShadowDancer realized what she did and vanished quickly into the shadows again slipping away she hoped undetected.

"That was too close." she whispered to herself, "and foolish."

She pulled herself back to ShadowKeep and appeared from the shadows as ShadowDancer. She bowed graciously to Hans, "HonorLord, I am at you service. May fortunes favor the just in the days ahead."

"You grace our halls. It is an honor to accept your favor for the people of Shadowkeep and Shadow Valley." Hans returned a flourishing bow.

She turned to the rest and before sitting stated her role in events. "I shall travel the shadows and give sanctuary to those less fortunate caught in the off scoring of events. Where I can and shall also avenge the destruction of the life of the land." her anger showed for a moment in her flames.

"For tonight, let us leave tomorrow from our thoughts, tomorrow will have enough thought for itself." Eric drew a swallow from his goblet.

"Hans," ShadowDancer whispered, "Your friends from the northern continent regret that they had not sent you assistance."

"You are here, and we have sufficient strength to defend against any threat." HonorLord stated with confidence.

Darval looked intently at his goblet, "Necromancers rely on what is not seen to win their battles."

CHAPTER 8

Cards Played

Jahaln did not know why Jaharadan was pacing so hard. "What troubles you, Master?"

"They do not know; they really do not know where Darval vanished to. Not even the leaders of the remnant of his people have an idea how to call to Darval or where he might have gone." Jaharadan stopped pacing and sat on the chest by the table in their tent. "The entire dark council has vanished, and I was expecting to use their favor to sway the decision to accept I was powerful enough to be counted among them."

"Surely your power is enough there will be no choice to accept you even without having favor. There are rules that must be observed." Jahaln looked out at the ocean, "You could stop right now and by the simple fact you have caused such a stir you can claim your rightful place."

"The claim would be weak. I may be keeping the other Ancients preoccupied around the world of Ethar with the stirring and laid a sizable threat at the door of a weaker Ancient, they could still discredit my success. If I can defeat one, I will have assured my place.'"

"I deffer to your wisdom, Master." Jahaln would play his part. He would keep to himself the thoughts he had. He was not in a position to walk away from Jaharadan and did not know if he ever would be. Unlike the Ancients Jaharadan could not sense where other Ancients were, but this worked to his advantage too, because they could not sense him that way yet either.

Jaharadan looked in the shallow basin of mercury, "Our troops are all moving as scheduled." He suddenly took a deeper interest in the basin, "What was that?"

"What, Master?"

"Something just burned to ash a hole in the middle of our skeletal armies, but I can detect nothing in the area."

"Perhaps they triggered a trap of some kind? Perhaps the ancient you challenge is more powerful than you expected? Or maybe one of the skeletal magi made a mistake?" Jahaln maintained his practiced disinterest, although he was very curious what might have happened.

"When they reach halfway down the central valley, we will move to a barren area on the eastern mountain ridge. We should be able to observe better from there without having to see across the ocean water." Jaharadan was referring to how ocean water can make it more difficult to scry. "Perhaps as you put it, I will be able to see what happened after we move."

"Perhaps, and perhaps we will have more room to move too." Jahaln stood and walked to the door. There really was no room outside their tent to walk. Movement caught his attention and he looked towards the mainland. "Dragon"

"Dragon? Why did I not know there were dragons here? No matter we proceed as planned. Dragons normally stay out of the battles of the Ancients."

*   *   *   *   *

"We have received a great blessing from the goddess ShadowDancer." Terriala started out after Samuel's introduction to the crowd that overflowed the clearing. "Many of you have enjoyed the harvest from this blessing and we have shared our excitement with each other. It is wonderful to rejoice with each other in excitement, and song to our goddess, but I beseech you all not to share word or explanation of this blessing with those who are not followers of ShadowDancer."

A murmur passed through the crowd in waves, Samuel raised his hands calling them back to order. "Listen to our High Priestess, she speaks with wisdom for our good. Would you have others learn our skill and join us to use our goddess, or use us and our gift for their own profiteering?"

They went silent, "I will confer with ShadowDancer and let you know her words." Terriala held up the flaming staff, "Until we have word to the contrary from the goddess be cautious what you let others know of her gifts. They will still see that the goddess is making us prosper and they will see that we take care of others in need, not just our own." As she brought the staff down, the lanterns around the clearing lit up. "Enjoy the feast and the company."

Samuel helped her down from the platform. "You did well."

"We are not all of ShadowDancer's followers, I just hope that other followers have the wisdom to use caution."

"You worry too much about things outside of your control." Samuel chuckled, "How many" he waved his hand in the direction of the gathering, "have any idea how much we can do with this gift?"

"I don't know," she slipped the gold sphere out of her pocket taking his hand and pressing it into his palm, "do you?" She watched him as he looked at the sphere and then registered what it was, eyes opening slightly. "I know I don't have any idea how much we can do."

He had trouble articulating any sound, "How ..."

"It really was a simple blessing. *'You need not carry a burden as you travel. The land will yield her bounty for you.'* That was it."

The unrestrained meaning of what the priestess was saying was starting to unfold in his mind. He found his voice again, "We have much to be thankful for and we have been trusted with more power than I would trust myself with."

"And I have one more thing I must show you but let us slip inside one of the tents. I hesitate to show anyone, but I need you to know."

"What more can there be?" he whispered as they slipped into the nearest tent.

"Place your hand on the ground, then just like you would summon fruit on a tree, summon a crystal from the ground in the shape of a symbolic heart."

He looked at her and hesitated, then followed her instructions and a ruby heart grew up out of the ground next to his hand. "We can not only grow that which is living, but the very elements of the land and we can shape them?" He sat on the ground, so as not to fall even from his squatted position.

"We have been given great hidden power." She stated as she pulled the dagger she had grown from inside her robes. It was a simple dagger, but what it symbolized was immense.

Samuel balanced the blade in his palm as he looked at it, "Is there a cost?"

"I don't know, and I don't know how long we shall have this gift either. It may go away as soon as we are no longer required to scout the lands. We were not given limits, nor do we have a way of knowing what would be abusing this wonderful gift. We only have our conscience to be our guide."

"We also don't know who can do how much or if what we can do varies between us. Perhaps this night we should all stockpile some reserves from what we can summon as a practical preparation for the days ahead?"

"There may be wisdom in letting that whisper spread. I would not tell anyone what we can do though. It is probably better to let them do what they figure out they can do on their own. As for me, this place here in the forest seems an appropriate place for a place of respect for ShadowDancer. I am going to see what I can do."

Samuel had in his own mind the things he wanted to do while he could and watched her leave into the shadows of the trees on the west side of the clearing before spreading whispers in the crowd and heading off to do his own thing. Terriala went to the smaller clearing just west of the large one and knelt on the ground placing both her hands in front of her. She envisioned a statue of ShadowDancer on a pedestal growing up out of the ground, blending stone and metal and gems to give it color and the appearance of life. The statue was slightly larger than life. When she finished the statue, she started her bigger project behind it. The more she did, the more she imagined she could do.

*   *   *   *   *

The winds were blowing from the east. This is a good thing. HonorLord, Hans, was starting to get comfortable with the title, thought to himself. Away from the Deamorg who could follow a scent, towards the humans of the southern kingdoms and the skeletons to the northwest. Skeletons cannot smell anything, and the union of the southern kingdoms were still a long way off even if they could pick up a scent. He signaled to raise the standard of ShadowKeep high and then lowered it. He watched the horsemen of Pendril raise their standard and lower it. The leader of the Dark Elf army raised and lowered his scepter. They all were in motion.

He had considered using the technique they had learned from ShadowDancer to be with all of the armies at the same time, but he had not been practicing and he needed to keep his center and focus. He would use the skill if and when he needed it. Scouts went ahead and he rode with the first battalion. It would be days before they met the actual enemy, so they moved at a conservative pace knowing the enemy was also moving towards them. As Ancient of War, he knew the movements of the enemy's armies and as a matter of course the abilities of his own armies were enhanced just because he was there. Narcole, a Dark Elf counsel given him by Darval rode by his side. Narcole had not been with HonorLord and ShadowKeep for long yet Hans felt like he knew him and Narcole would stay with him and teach him the ways of the Dark Elves and as an emissary after the wars were over. Narcole knew who and what HonorLord was, after all he was one of Darval's top ministers, governing the militant followers.

"It almost doesn't seem fair." HonorLord commented.

"What would that be, My lord?" Narcole responded.

"I was thinking aloud, but we go into battle holding all the aces," he paused mid-sentence, "advantages. I know the movements of the enemy, I know their strengths and weaknesses, and I can tilt the scales of every fight."

"We fight an enemy that is led by one who would exalt himself into the ranks of the Ancients through the blood of many." Narcole showed no expression, "Would you have it any other way, other than to crush him utterly in his cause?"

"I absolutely agree. It was merely an observation."

"I am not good at esoteric pondering and philosophy."

"There is a clearing about an hour ahead." HonorLord boomed forth, "We shall camp there for the night." Runners went forth and spread the word.

*   *   *   *   *

Jahaln followed Jaharadan as they sped across the water towards the mainland. They needed to move closer as the armies marched deeper. They were stepping up from the beach into the forest within minutes of leaving the island. Once they were under cover, Jaharadan slowed to a fast walk. "We want to remain undetected. We will travel the cracks in the stone of the Eastern Mountain Ridge. There are some caves to the south where we will watch events unfold."

"I am with you, Master." Jahaln followed into the ravines, keeping his focus on controlling the movements of the armies he had been instructed to orchestrate. Jahaln had never actually been here before, but knew where they were from the memories, he had gained from Jaharadan. He knew where they were going as they wove through the rocky landscape rarely exposed, keeping cover to avoid being seen by any wandering eyes.

They stopped ducking down against the wall in the small ravine under and out cropping of rock overhead. They both could sense the dragon swooping closer. It flew directly over them from the side of the ravine they were crouched against and they watched as it passed by. "They are searching, but not for food. Perhaps I underestimated the involvement of the dragons."

"She was looking too close to be trying to track the movements of an army. Do you think they are searching for us?" A part of Jahaln was hoping they would be found. He wanted riches and power, but not at the price that would be paid. He pushed these thoughts back deep inside; he could not let even the scent of such contrary thoughts slip out to Jaharadan.

"Ah, well, the better for our cause." Jaharadan sneered, "The more effort that is put into stopping us the greater the measure of my worthiness to be recognized as an Ancient."

"Isn't power stronger without the glory." avoiding the glaring gaze of the lich, Jahaln quickly continued, "I mean as an unknown power you can bring about many changes without opposition. The more known you are the more you will be watched for what you might be doing, and so your results may not be as great."

Jaharadan turned to press ahead, "There is some wisdom to your thinking, but once you have the power, recognition also gives you credibility which in itself is power."

As they slipped down another ravine, Jahaln pondered these words. "The last ship has unloaded, and they are almost all to the shore now in the East. Their wills are strong, what if they break from the control of the blood-wine?"

"The battle will already be started, and the longtime enemies will fight it out after that even if we do lose control. Darval has long since abandoned his interest in this world and they are on their own."

They were close to their destination as they sped through the cracks in the stone mountainous ridges. "The skeleton and undead armies need no rest, but the necromancers running them do. They are at a good point to rest for the night master."

"Then give them their rest, I don't want them to fail for weariness." turning to enter the caves, "However, have them send scouts ahead so we can learn the movements of our enemies."

*   *   *   *   *

Darkness had filled a part of his soul since the loss of Stralina and he looked around his makeshift office a little disorientated for a moment. His heart was not as heavy as it would have been. He did not know if he had dreamed or actually visited this distant place until he reached down and found the ribbon tied around the hilt of his sword. He had been there; the place had been like an echo of Shadow Keep barely making itself known in a distant realm overlooking her world. He knew very little about her except that he felt the tug of her heart in his own.

Closing his eyes, their tender encounter had given renewed life to that which he had thought had died with his Jinn. He ached to be with her again, to be with her still. He had to focus; they were still at war. Demon fiends were still landing on the shores to the east, the kingdom to the south had been bent to the dark lords will and undead armies were still marching from the North-West in their direction. He slipped back out into the evening air.

Working his forms and katas, he regained his center; he would live to see her again. His blades sang through the air, mixed with bursts of speed turning him into a blur of darkness. As he drove his blades through his imaginary enemies the image of his fallen Stralina gave him commitment and fury, while the gentle reminder of the ribbon against his wrist gave him the strength of hope. He would do well in the battles to come and inspire his armies to do well with him. As he came to a stop ShadowBlade stood between his hands, the flat towards him, the ten thousand and more souls the blade drank in, now looked back. Perhaps after this war was won, he would quench the blade in the black fires that forged it and deliver those souls to rest. Should those souls be brought back again with new life, they would have no memory of the dark lives they led before.

HonorLord carefully sheathed his sword and stowed his gear safely in some rocks by the waterfall. The water felt good, cool against his skin already glistening wet blending into the darkness with the sweat of his workout. He let himself get lost in the showering water. There was time to consider all things, but for now he was just himself again enjoying the cleansing of the water.

The water ran down his body, rolling over his rippling muscles, cut and obviously powerful, but deceptively small for his real strength. A warm smile filled him as the thought of L'Akyra slipped through his mind. He wondered when he would see her again. He stood there letting the water of the small falls wash over him, feeling it clean his soul.

"Are you going to spend all night becoming one with a waterfall or shall we knock down some ale and chat about the impending doom?"

"Narcole, you have made it back!" grabbing his towel as he stepped from the falls almost invisible in the moonless night. "What news do you have for me?"

"Darval, asked again that we try not to go head-to-head with the Daemon legions, they are under the Liche's power and if we can eliminate the Liche, they will listen to him. He is still working on a way to break the enchantment also."

"If we go head-to-head, there will be major losses on both sides, but we are at war on three fronts, which does not give us a lot of room to back away."

"A contingency of mages went south ahead of the armies of Pendril to create a diversion and should be able to delay their armies for at least twelve days." Narcole said looking off in the night sky.

"We have to face off the undead armies; they are leaving a swath of destruction in their path, killing everything. Their numbers grow after each battle with the animation or reanimation of those who fall from both sides." Hans finished tying the last corded fastener on his vest. "We have split forces. You Dark Elves are faster and lighter on foot then the armor-clad forces of the rest of our armies. You also have skills at vanishing when you need to. You are better suited at leading the daemons on a chase without having to engage in hard conflict."

"HonorLord, skeletal scouts have been spotted half a day out." The messenger ran up handing a scroll to Hans. Hans opened the scroll and etched a symbol in the air above it reading as the text appeared. "The armies are to be roused in four hours and begin forming the battle lines." Etching a note, he handed the scroll back to the messenger and sent him on his way.

Hans turned back to Narcole, "Please give proper greetings to the commanders in our southern flank. I do not have time now to wait for an answer. You know what to do."

"I shall my friend. May the Ancients guide us well and bring us to the day of victory." Placing a hand on Hans' shoulder, "You will do well, until we meet again. I forget sometimes you are one of the Ancients."

They both turned to head their separate ways. Hans heard the strum of the distant bowstring and the arrow through the air. With lightning speed, he snatched the shaft out of the air before it reached Narcole's back. The coat of arms embossed on the back of Hans' Gauntlet slammed into Narcole's shoulder as he turned leaving a clear mark as if he were branded. The skeletal assassin came rushing down on Narcole, but ShadowBlade intercepted knocking the assassin's blade away and drinking the animated life out of the skeleton. The bones carried by momentum bounced off of Narcole's deflections before hitting the ground.

Narcole bowed deep to Hans, "HonorLord indeed, perhaps one day I shall be able to repay you this debt."

"A soldier has a life debt to every soldier who fights on the same side in battle, so we are even." Hans return the bow. "Now let us go defend each other's backs."

*　　*　　*　　*　　*

Bonny gazed out the window at the rebuilding that was still going on in Shadow Valley, extending her thoughts to help, or do something nice from time to time. What she was doing was keeping her mind off the battles there were impending until she was needed. "Eric, I am going to go through the medical facilities again. Yes, I know everything is ready, but I am going to check again anyway."

"Okay, hun," Eric looked up from enchanting another weapon to be used in the defense of ShadowKeep.

*　　*　　*　　*　　*

ShadowDancer sat in meditation in the chamber directly behind the throne. Her focus was elsewhere. She slipped through the shadows in five different directions. She monitored the approaching armies in all three directions, but what she was looking for was more subtle then the obvious for the impending battles. Splitting was becoming easier for her the more she did it. Three to watch the armies, one at ShadowKeep so she could be reached easily if needed and two out combing the continent for signs of the mastermind behind the current events.

ShadowDancer Swept north along the rocky coast, under other circumstances she would have enjoyed watching the ocean waves crashing against the lower reaches of the stone cliffs. Today she was searching and hiding to avoid being discovered in her search. Random things caught her eye pulling her attention to search harder only to find nothing abnormal for the location. She cataloged her findings in the back of her mind, gem deposits, metal veins, cliff monkeys, old ancient shipwrecks. For a moment she wondered why nobody had salvaged anything from the coast, but quickly realized the waters were just too dangerous.

She paused as the coastline turned more west then northward. She gazed to the north and felt a longing she was not familiar with. An ache pulsed through her to go home. It had been days now since she left and she was sure her mom and dad would be worried, not just about her, but about the events that were unfolding also. She would send Chareece home, but not right now. Soon she would send Chareece home, when she had a little more to let her family know.

Her eyes lifted to the sky and the stars reminded her of a tale told to her as a child about the ancient called the nine sisters. ShadowDancer wondered if this mythical ancient had also known the secret of dividing herself into multiple identities as she was doing right now. More than that it made her wonder how the rest of the ancients didn't already know how to do this. They had been around for thousands of years, but both Gaharias and Darval seemed to have never seen it done before. She would have to be more careful what she shared and with whom, perhaps some of what she could do would be best kept secret.

A voice called to her from out in the ocean to the north. ShadowDancer tried to push it aside thinking it was her homesick longing, but it called again. It was very weak, but the further along the coast she moved the stronger it got. The voice was not exactly calling her, it was just calling out. She turned towards the call. The waves of the open ocean offered a unique shifting of shadow and light. She adjusted easily but enjoyed the change from the things she was familiar with.

How do you betray a liche without letting them know you are calling for help? Simple really, you divide the inner-self from the outer-self and don't let your outer-self know what you are doing. Then you call out to the Ancients. If the liche answers you have proven he is an Ancient and you can celebrate and hope he does not see your intent. If not, then you wait and hope another Ancient hears your secret call.

The wisp of a presence on the rock in the middle of the ocean was almost to feint for ShadowDancer to see from the shadows. When she was certain that the wisp like essence was alone on the rock she stepped out of the shadows. She was answering a call to the Ancients and the knowledge of events around the call were there as they always are. ShadowDancer touched the wisp like form and gave it strength to communicate with her. "You left a day ago?"

"Indeed, we travel inland to a cave where we are to orchestrate the armies of war."

"You wish me to stop your master."

"He seeks to be elevated to being recognized as an Ancient and I should rejoice at the wealth it will deliver to me, but what good is all the treasure of the world if the world despises you?"

"You are bound to the Liche; you may suffer the same fate."

"I shall accept the fate I have earned."

*   *   *   *   *

Merlin sat in meditation also. He sat in the gardens communing with the plants and with the birds that flew in and out. The Liche was on the continent, he passed with another into the rocks of the astern ridges to the north. It was another opportunity missed, but he let the others at ShadowKeep know what he knew. The plants and creatures of the fields became distracted with the path of death being left by the Liche's armies. Merlin felt the shuddering of the land at the movement of the army. The power of the goddess and the Lady of the Lake were failing to give him good information from the land.

"Hello Merlin." ShadowDancer had left off her meditation to find out from others any news. "What are you doing here in the garden?"

"You listen to the shadows; I listen to the voices of the plants and animals." He looked up with a smile. He had surmised she had a way of listening to shadows to gain her knowledge and voiced it not knowing he just planted a concept in her mind.

"Have you learned anything from these voices." *voices of shadows* she considered what he unintentionally suggested. *Are there voices in the shadows, perhaps a life to the shadows she could hear?*

"No words of what we seek. I see the armies coming, but no sign of their leader. It is as if they are hiding from nature."

"It is in the nature of necromancy to hide from what is natural, isn't it?" ShadowDancer sent a whisper to the shadows and felt the shadows move in response.

"I suppose there is truth to that." He rolled out a map on the bench next to where he was sitting, "There are areas were not much nature or otherwise lives, the two biggest being the path of the necromancy armies and the Eastern Mountain Ridge stretching along the north eastern portion of the continent." He pointed on the map as he referred to each area.

"I am searching up the eastern coast and monitoring the movements of the armies." She could feel the strain of being in six places at once, she needed more time to master this. Each additional split seemed to be more difficult than the one before. "I should go back to my meditation."

"The course of events has already been cast." Merlin stated almost to himself. "We each have our parts as events unfold." He returned his focus to his commune with the plants and animals there were selections among those he saved that he would return to the Lady of the Lake and they would gladly serve Bridget. Unlike the ancients of Ethar, she got her strength from the believing of her followers and their love of the land.

*　　*　　*　　*　　*

Delmar was on the outskirts of the followers of ShadowDancer. He was not there when she declared her priestess, nor were any of his group of followers. "We have been given these wonderful gifts, so we do not need to be down trodden and less favored anymore."

Peltricia nodded her agreement, "So why should we have to hide our increase?"

"We can build our own village here. We do not need to keep migrating looking for work and service we can provide others." Delmar knew they were not far from the road to Harmosk. "Nobody has actually explored this are before, so there will be little suspicion when it is 'discovered'. We can build everything we want." He freely pulled lumber form the trees around him. "Then we can harvest and sell supplies from our village instead of someone else's farm and them getting all the profits."

The others with them cheered the idea. Peltricia held up her hand quieting the crowd, there were twenty-eight present if you only counted the adults. "Each of us has discovered different abilities of things we can do, but between us we can supply everything we need to make this a great village and place to stop and raise our families."

"We do not have to follow the self-appointed priestess and leader of ShadowDancer's followers. We followed her without them, and we can continue to do so without bending to their whim to keep hidden our gifts." Delmar stated as one who had authority, having led this small band for several years now.

"This does not mean," Peltricia added, "that we have any need to be hostile or make enemies out of the followers who who accept their priestess. We are just a separate group from them. As long as they do not try to impose their will on us we will do the same."

They all agreed and began laying out markers and making their plans for their village. When it was complete, they would build a road connected to the road to Harmosk. They will be self-sufficient now and would welcome travelers and govern their own lives.

*　　*　　*　　*　　*

Hans made it quickly back to the makeshift command post. "Wake everyone and make ready now! An assassin has slipped through our line, who knows what else has gotten through. The battle is already upon us."

Those with magic skills began casting protections and illusions, hiding troops from the undead and laying in traps. Healers were scattered through the ranks and a medical camp was set up behind the lines. Blue glows flickered through the forests and battle lines as detection spells were cast and the scattered skirmish as undead were discovered that had slipped through.

Everything slipped into silent waiting and after a short period of time a messenger made their way back to the command tent. "Almost 200 had slipped into our ranks, HonorLord. They have been eliminated and we only lost twenty men sir."

"We did good!" General Duncan commented not elated at loosing men but finding the odds favorable for a surprise attack.

"We have to do much better." Hans looked around the table at the commanding ranks seated with him. "They outnumber us three thousand to one. One to ten was a successful attack for them. Their goal is to wear us down." As if on cue they all began to hear the rustling sound still hours away of the shear masses of undead moving on their position. Hans pulled two small stones from a pocket and held them up. One turned into a small shadowy dragon and the other into a bird. Both of the animated messengers vanished in flight. "It was a dragon that once told me, 'If you burned your dead necromantic magic would have nothing to animate.' There is some wisdom in his words."

The generals all stood with him looking at the direction the sound was coming from. General Arcalneron stepped forward. "It will be better if I go down and fight with my men now then standing back here watching." The others nodded agreement heading off leaving Hans standing alone with a handful of messengers. He remembered the elves that fought for the defense of the Uklian and wished they could be here this day too. They were even now defending their lands again from the threat of the same lich. The lich was a very powerful necromancer who never died but is no longer really living. He is sustained by his magic and is said to have enough power that he claims himself to have become one of the Ancients.

Hans knew that there had to have been at the least several Arch-Necromancers in service to this lich in order for him to be fighting wars on four continents. He also knew because of the nature of the evil rivalry, in the end there could only be one Arch Necromancer serving one Liche Lord. The Arch Necromancers would be seen though, and the Liche Lord or dark lord would remain hidden unless he was forced to reveal himself.

Hans touched his chest and leaped into the air taking the form of a dragon with wings spread. He headed straight towards the sound of the approaching undead armies, staying close to the treetops to avoid being seen before he passed overhead. Taking a deep breath and spewing flames as soon as he started passing over the skeletal ranks. The army was massive, arching his flight to the right; he never did see the end of the masses. There were no enemies in the air, this was good. There was no count for the number of enemies left scorched, but it may have compensated for the odds of the infiltration. He landed safely on his feet back in the command camp transforming back as he landed.

Timing was everything; the troops would stave off the first waves of skeletons with relative ease. Hundreds at a time would get dispelled by the holy casters, but then they would have to start reserving their power for healing and stamina. If everything goes as planned this is about when the Dragons will sweep over each using their breath weapons, fire, ice, acid or whatever their best attack was sweeping over the enemy. Then the Giant Rocs would follow dropping boulders and debris smashing the enemies or picking them up and dropping them on each other.

This sweep would boost morale and give the troops restored zeal for battle. It would also draw out whatever tricks the enemy might have up their sleeves as counter measures. If the enemy was prepared for an air battle, he did not want to exhaust his airborne army prematurely. The dragons and Rocs would take a brief rest waiting to see what might arise.

Hans watched as the first wave of skeletons never reached the front lines, cut down by casting and banishing. With the second wave, the casters began their rotation so that they could keep their powers regenerated about a third of the second wave of skeletons reached the lines to be cut down relatively easy. Skeletons were not good in battle, but once in a while one would get a lucky hit. As casters turned to mending wounds and boosting endurance or re-enforcing defensive measures, about half of the third wave of skeletons made it to the battle lines.

He watched carefully, the next wave was Zombies and other undead creatures. They did not run fast, but they did not tire and were harder to take down then skeletons. Their sole purpose was to wear down troops. He watched as his horsemen moved out from the right and left flanks to comb the lands and protect the main force from ambushes from the sides. The second wave of zombies and mixed undead creature started sweeping down and Hans sent up a flare signal and the entire wave was consumed by the fire trap that had been laid. The flames also cleared the fields of undead corpses. Mage winds pushed the forest fires into the enemy ranks.

The droning of drumbeats began from further back in the enemy ranks, forcing more casters to use their magic against the demoralizing magic of the enemy. The drums of battle and trumpets began among his ranks. Undead armies are powerful by their sheer numbers. They do not think as individuals and their strategies are only as good as the Necromancer or necromancers that are controlling them. There are only two ways to stop the army, kill every one of them or kill the necromancer controlling them.

An army this size is bound to also have summoned undead liches and summoned daemons. The undead liches may persist on their own for a little while after the Necromancer is dead and the daemons have a short time before their summoning dispels. The daemons are the key though to finding the Necromancer. If the necromancer made a mistake with one of the daemon and sent them to defeat an enemy instead of fight an enemy, they can be used to find the necromancer. A daemon sent on a task that it cannot accomplish will turn on the summoner and can be followed back to find the necromancer.

The next wave was more of the mix and a few casters throwing decay spells into the ranks. This sent more troops back to the medical camp. It was time for him to boost moral by deed. Hans used light-weaving and light-walked into the front of the battle lines. He made sure he was seen by the troops and accelerated as he stepped into battle, single-handed cutting down half of the 6th wave before light-stepping back to the command post.

He saw what was coming next and sent runners to the catapults and archers. The undead ogres and trolls and giants were easily twice the size they had been when they were alive. The catapults and archers launched fires as the wave approached. Flaming oil and magic arrows seemed at first to have no effect but they started collapsing as they reached the line causing more damage dyeing then the previous waves of enemies had caused, forcing the lines to pull back. The daemons looked like bats in the distance taking to the air and Hans quickly sent signal to the dragons and Rocs. The aerial battle met above the battlefield, limiting the use of catapults and archery to counter the approaching giant undead.

The lines were forced back, and the command post was forced back to the secondary position. Hans took dragon form again so that he could follow the battle. The flying daemons were shredded by the dragons and Rocs with minimal loss, but they served their intended purpose forcing his line of defense back. The Wave was defeated, but the next one was on its way. Hans signaled the charge and forced the lines back forwards, while the dragons and Rocs took care of most of the next wave.

Hans was getting concerned, while they were winning wave after wave of battle, they still had no idea where the necromancer or necromancers were. Without taking out the necromancers, this army could be rebuilt while they were off fighting somewhere else. He sent the Rocs on reconnaissance to search the lands and the Dragons to search the remainder of the armies coming down on them, randomly spewing balls of fire. Hans noticed that the dragons turned their fallen brethren and the fallen Rocs to ashes before leaving the battlefield.

The next wave was a mix of everything that had come before and the ranks were also filled with phantoms and ghosts. Hans had anticipated this and made sure that every blade had at least some type of enchantment on it and every piece of armor also. Ghosts and phantoms can only be hit by magical weapons and the only protection is magical armor.

They were winning and the battle was not too far from over, perhaps another five waves. They had suffered losses and so far, nothing was found to stop them from having the same battle again in a week. Hans had followed the rules of the ancients although he had never been given any official recognition or status as one. These were his people he was not going to have them fight to victory so that they could keep doing it over and over until there were not enough left to win. He captured the space of time between moments.

In the space between moments, you can see the threads that join things together and he followed those threads to the source of the enemy armies. He found twelve necromancers laughing and pointing towards the battle. They were inside a dome that was concealing them, a dome that was made of fabric only the ancients are supposed to be able to manipulate. Either the lich had become an ancient or was working with one. The source of the dome was the amulets around the necromancer's necks, linked to somewhere way north. He was guessing all the way up to the Northlands Continent where the lich was running his wars.

Hans took the daggers of each of the necromancers and used the hands of the necromancers next to them to plunge the daggers in a circle of death. He slipped back to his command camp and released the moment. He had saved his people and ended this battle and now stood watching as the last of the battle played out. The hosts and phantoms vanished. The remainder of the enemy armies collapsed or vanished. A cheer went up through the troops. Hans felt like somehow, he had gotten his hands dirty.

The report came back that twelve necromancers were found dead, apparently, they killed each other. It took a full day to Pile all the undead corpses and burn them to ashes along with the necromancers and everything on them. They cleaned up what they could; nature would have to take care of the rest. He looked over the landscape. He had saved lives, saved the land from greater destruction. He did something he was sure was good but felt guilty about it. He had killed thousands in battle without any sense of guilt. He always fought for what he thought was right. This still felt like he did something wrong. He felt like a dark seed had been planted in his soul.

His hand touched the ribbon on the hilt of his sword; a sense of hope dispelled his despair. He mounted up and began the march back to Shadow Keep. They would make it home before home was under siege. If things went according to plan the dark elves should arrive one day behind them and neither the daemons nor the armies of the southern kingdom could penetrate Shadow Keep. The army of beasts coming from the west would be slow at getting there and be as likely to do as much damage to the attacking armies as they were to anything else. As long as they were all focused on Shadow Keep the rest of the land would be safe.

*　　*　　*　　*　　*

Shiheel let both of the Dark Elves have free run in his shop, after all they were sent by the Ancient Darval to assist him in finding the antidote or cure for the blood elixir being used for mind control. "Chemically we have countered the elixir, which will remove the toxins from the imbibers of the mind control potion. This will remove the physical effects that were making it easier for the magics to put them in the deathlike state that allows for the necromantic mind control, but we have not identified the precise magic being used."

Hesheil placed a magic orb around Makeir his pet monkey, "I have recorded the effects of the neutralized potion on Makeir already. I have made the assumption that this will be necromantic since in fact our enemy is a lich, sustained by the same type of magic." He turned to one of the dark elves, "Chardone, cast one at a time each spell you know to bring Makeir to that state of living dead, which would allow for mind control. At the very least removing the toxin effects will make it more difficult for them to control as many. We could send what we have as a start."

Relkauff VeeDeuarin his brother piped in, "I am still going to continue working on a counter for the mind control itself. If we can beat that out directly the results will be quicker and more effective."

Chardone began casting, "I agree with you in part brother, but that would also require powerful casters spread out everywhere to work the counter-spells, Shiheel is right that this will permanently liberate the victims with a mist that can be delivered once and does not require a continued application to counter the effect."

"Are you saying give up?"

"No, having both would be best. I am sure there is a need to be able to do an immediate counter even if it is not permanent." Chardone added with a rather viscous sneer, "besides we can add all of this to our collection of knowledge when we return home." Relkauff snickered.

"That was it, that last spell was a perfect match." Hesheil repeated the cast that Chardone had just used and confirmed the results were the same.

"If you can cast our magic why did you need me to do it?"

"Chardone, I just learned that when you cast it, I have no previous knowledge of your castings, although some I am sure overlap the knowledge I have." Hesheil replied.

"You are a very dangerous people." Relkauff commented the implications were not lost on how easily this new race could absorb all of their knowledge if they had access. "I have done it." He leaned over the glowing orb and cast again, "Indeed, it works, it actually takes a combination of counter magic, mind blocking and freewill casting, then a cleansing heal spell to remove the residuals." He used a magic quill and scribed the scroll in the air. "If we combine this with the mist you are working on we should be able to effectively remove the control and prevent it from coming back, even if they are forced to drink again."

*　　*　　*　　*　　*

Lord Rolland and the mounted forces started in motion with the lowering of the pendant to meet an enemy that was over a week's march away. The first day's ride they pressed hard, everyone had to walk their horses down and brush them well at the end of the day. The majority of the horsemen were from Pendril, however there was a good number from Shadowkeep and not a few from among the dark elves of the shadow world. They slept with their horses. The squads and regiments were divided according to the groups they were familiar fighting with, live battle of this nature did not seem to be the right time to work on new relationships with strangers in battle. Near the end of the second day the lead scouts came back reporting the armies of the southern kingdoms were sighted ahead making camp.

"So, Hansen you say they all appear to be in good spirits, but currently not to aware or alert to any danger?" Rolland inquired.

"Yes, Sir." the scout answered, "I think I could have ridden right in their midst and they would have welcomed me as a comrade as long as they did not recognize our emblem. They already have a mix from the various kingdoms, different flags, different colors."

Rolland turned to the leaders from the separate divisions, "Our mission is to cause division, reduce their numbers and slow them down. We want to do our best to get them to turn around and go home and avoid direct involvement in the battle at ShadowKeep. We need our best rogues to slip in and retrieve symbols and arrows, anything that can be identified as from the ranks of one group to use against another." Rolland paused while messengers were sent back."

One of the night elf leaders, Treslicden, "When the rogues have returned, we will begin casting enchantments of paranoia on their camps, it should increase the level of panic when we strike."

Rolland nodded in acknowledgment, "Two hours after dark we strike, quick, release as much incriminating evidence using their arrows and dropping items. Fire a minimal number of shots as effective as you can and vanish back into the woods. They should not follow for two reasons, first they will be caught by surprise, second for fear of being lured into an ambush. We will rendezvous a mile back and on the north side of the trail they have blazed with their march."

The plans were already laid out for how they would move into position and attack the enemy camps from both sides. They would sneak in as close as they could undetected, then strike and vanish. The objective was not to kill anyone, but rather to cause injury significant to require down time for individuals and at least one other to care for them. One out of five carried arrows that would burst into flames when they hit, of course the primary targets for them would be supplies.

Phase one passed with no alarms and no casualties and the arrows and items were distributed. What was used for each attack would be from a neighboring camp or group. Rolland took his small party of about 36 horsemen against the middle of the lead enemy camp. They road up casually to minimize the noise until they could see the fires and lights of the camp. From what they could see each was given a target location to attack and ride straight back away from the camp.

They charged in, each firing two or three shots and turning around and racing away before anyone in the camp was on their feet to fend them off. They vanished into the woods, reformed and headed north to circle around to where they would meet the rest. They could hear the raucous that was caused a mile away as they slipped through the night. The light of the night was good enough to be sure of their trail, but dark enough to conceal their identity.

After everyone had reported, Rolland concluded that things went much better than expected. The first strike was complete. Everyone had successfully launched three shots, significant damage and injury was done and no one on their side sustained even an injury from the encounter. According to scouts the camps were segregating and posting guards between camps.

"We have done well everyone. Keep guards posted and get what sleep we can, we are up again in 6 hours, before the light of day." They were all trained to go days without sleep, but they would rotate who got shorted sleep each night. Not all slept, some stood guard, others scouted their perimeter and others still ran scouting around the enemy camps. Rolland was up reading the night reports when the early morning reports started coming in.

In the middle of the night a contingent of the enemy headed back the way they came, abandoning the main force, they would not be pursued. There were random skirmishes between camps, but no major fighting. There were enough disturbances to keep the armies from getting any reasonable sleep. The regiment leaders were gathered when he stepped out. He chewed a piece of hardtack and one of dried fruit as he addressed them. Each of them carried two weeks hard rations in saddle bags. "Ready your lightening squads remember rotate quick strikes and out, then the next squad. They will have to clam-shell to defend and then we will break off attacks and rest. They cannot move while clam-shelled for defense." He lifted his water skin up and they all lifted a fist up in response. "When they set their defenses, we will move ahead of them several miles, lay traps and rest while we wait for them to start moving again."

Rolland led the third strike, six horsemen racing close enough to fire their bows once, maybe twice and vanishing again. A few random shots were fired in their direction, a saddle bag was hit and a close call stuck in a quiver, but none of them were hurt, although whole group had sustained a couple minor injuries. They were lucky and he knew it. The enemy camp began to tighten in, archers taking cover in positions to shoot as the horsemen approached, so they stopped attacking. And headed five miles ahead in the direction towards ShadowKeep and laid traps for the impending approach. The traps were designed to injure not to kill, an injury takes two or three out of battle while killing only take out one. Also, injury would slow down their movement.

Scouts reported back that the Southern army was not moving. Everyone took shifts resting or waiting. The night passed and morning came. The sun had been up a few hours before the first report came that the Army of the southern kingdoms was breaking camp. Their own horsemen were patrolling their flanks, although their numbers were not great enough to keep a shield up the full length of the army, they did increase the danger to using the lightning strike small groups. When it came time, they would have to attack in larger groups and target any riders first.

The riders from ShadowKeep were a good mile the other side of where the traps started and mounted when the first signal trap let them know the armies were approaching and exactly where. The traps were doing their job, the massive army was slowed waiting for scouts to run ahead and scour the land for more traps. The dark elves lead the waves in the next raid attacks, casting spells with the singular purpose of spooking the horse and rendering the defending horsemen useless so the archers could target wagon drivers and the flaming arrows could target supplies. The southern army ground to a halt again taking a defensive posture and the horsemen stopped attacking. Any members that fell behind or headed back home were left alone by the horsemen. As long as they were not moving or moving slow enough the horsemen of ShadowKeep did not attack.

The army sent a small contingent ahead to scout and none returned. The members were stripped of everything except minimal clothing and a few daggers and left miles behind the army to find their way home. The armor was used to make animated apparitions that effectively put the army even more on edge. Internal fighting increased and a few of the different banners turned and left heading back towards their homes.

Enough traps were laid ahead, to force them to keep slowing down and searching. Mages enjoyed animating objects and sending them out as distractions while lightning strikes attacked form maximum ranges. When the barony forces moved their defenses to the rear, they would attack the front, when they moved to defend the front, they would attack the rear.

*   *   *   *   *

ShadowDancer could feel the threads of life from the dieing elf adoma near the edge of the trail of destruction left by the undead armies. She almost missed it because the young elf girl was well hidden, and spells cast to keep her from being found. The young girl was the only survivor from the small village. Her being there did explain why the adoma had not vanished completely. Using her true sight, ShadowDancer could see her curled up in the remnants of a shelter within feet of the line of destruction.

ShadowDancer knelt in front of the young girl, "What is your name?"

"You see me?" the young girl said suppressed fear in her eyes.

"I see you; we need to get you out of here to someplace safe." ShadowDancer reached out a hand, "Come tell me your name while I get you to somewhere safe. Do you have family anywhere else?"

The girl reached up with both hands looking over her shoulder at the vast destruction, "I am Leleshi. Is the evil gone? Are you part of the evil?"

"I am here to help. I will take you where you will be safe. I think I know who can watch over you until I can come get you." With a thought they went to a place where the young elf would be safe and ShadowDancer returned alone after making arrangements.

Who else or what else might still be lost out here? She sped along the edge of the trail of destruction looking for those things not readily visible. The path of destruction was terrible, the land might never look the same. She kept her focus on finding any living creatures that might need help.

She was still in six places and needed to pull at least one back, she was determined that anything that needed help along the path of the undead could not wait until she could get back. She was not going to stop monitoring the armies with Hans and Narcole, not pull back from the Dark Elfs and daemons playing cat and mouse, she was closing in on the position of the lich and she had to keep her place in ShadowKeep to report back what she saw. Lord Rolland and the horsemen were doing well, and she did not feel that she needed to keep monitoring them for now. She could always take another look after one of her other tasks was complete.

Meditating at Shadow Keep, she learned that the shadows really did answer. This would take time to master, shadows do not think the same as light, they did not see color and she actually had to slip into shadow form before they would really cooperate with her at all. After working with them for a while, she changed back to her form. It was going to take time to understand how they thought and communicated, too long to be of benefit today. She was sure that she would be able to make her own shadow minions to do bidding for her. Somehow, she picked up that information from the shadows that were willing to touch her in shadow form.

There he was the Liche; she could report his location.

CHAPTER 9

Tattered the Threads

Terriala called to Samuel to follow her to what she had been working on. "Isn't she perfect?" She asked as they stepped into the small clearing.

Samuel was impressed, "Indeed, have you been working on things all night?"

"That is not important." She caught his hand and lead him into the entrance of the cave. It went down about twelve steps and opened into a good size chamber with benches along the walls. There were shelves in the walls that had survival equipment and space for other supplies. "Now this is important." She stepped to the back wall and pushed on one of the stones. A section of the wall opened. They stepped through again into a passage with walls made from the rare metal of the mountains. It was only about six paces long and opened into a room with walls, floor and ceiling all metal. There were benches, hooks on the walls, shelves and tables in the large room. On the opposite wall three entryways lead to long rooms and he could see they were filled with weapons and armor in wall racks.

"This is amazing, and you must have stayed up all night to get this all done. Are there any more secrets to expose?"

Terriala laughed, "At least one." She lifted the top of the nearest bench and it opened into a chamber filled with coins and gems.

He picked up one of the coins. It was a small twenty-piece gold coin. On one side was an image of the goddess and on the other was her seal, the lion with the flame and the wreath of peace. There was a full variety of coins, silver, gold, copper and even some platinum. "Are all of the benches full?"

"Of course. This place is to remain a secret though unless we should need it. Knowledge to pass on to the next in line as priest and leader only."

"The secret is safe with me." He pulled one of each coin from the bench, "We want to be consistent in what we make." they headed out and closed the hidden opening before stepping out of the cave.

"There is so much more we can do." Terriala Knelt down and touched the vines by the cave and they grew over concealing the entrance. "To start with we should distribute a small amount of coinage to everyone, so that we can pay our way when we pass through a village. I would encourage everyone to continue to provide services, such as gardening, maintenance and prove our value without letting on what we can do. Spread the word."

Melina showed up just as Samuel was leaving. "Hello, priestess of ShadowDancer, and sister."

Terriala turned to see Melina floating next to the statue, "Hello, messenger of ShadowDancer and my sister."

"Nice statue."

"Do you think our goddess will like it?"

"I am sure ShadowDancer will appreciate what you have done, including what you have hidden. The threat of the new religion seems to be backing off some and the real battle is on another continent. ShadowDancer has gone there for a short while to help. All you have to do is call if you need her and she has given me some freedom to help with some things for her."

"It is hard to tell sometimes, sister if you are dead or somehow alive. We buried your body, but I see you and can touch you when you come on her bidding."

"I am dead sister, I only live within her, I have no breath in this world of my own." she faded and became insubstantial, "Would it be easier for you if I came like this?"

"No, please. Forgive me I was not complaining, just pondering that you, never mind," she held back tears, "I just miss you, do not punish me for that. I accept the fate we have chosen and thank our goddess she has seen fit to lets us in her grace even though we were foolish."

Melina returned to full substance and gave her sister a hug, "Perhaps it would be easier for you if I were not your sister and you could mourn and find your way passed your grief?"

"No, Melina, I will work it out. I will attend to my mourning and grief and accept things as they are. Give my time and I will come to peace and let us keep this gift that ShadowDancer has given you and I."

"I will give you time. I love you my sister and if seeing me causes you hurt, it will be I who requests of our goddess to send another when dealing with you. I will give you time first. My soul aches when I cause you pain."

"Let ShadowDancer know we have seen no further sign of the cult in the south lands. Let her know that her people have been helping the towns and villages rebuild."

"Stay in peace, priestess of ShadowDancer."

*   *   *   *   *

Rengelaqk led the dark elves toward the coast. They were four days out and Darval had not prepared him for what they saw. The legions number in the thousands, easily five times the fifteen hundred Dark Elf brethren that were here with him. At least they were not supposed to face this massive army toe to toe, only distract them for a while, leading a game of chase up and down the coastal regions.

They split into three forces the leaders of each group were psionically linked so they could precisely track each other's movements and keep an open communication. One third went around the southern end of the enemy forces, one third went around the northern end Rengelaqk waited with the other third until all were in place. With a silent command, the southern flank proceeded with an antagonizing attack followed by a retreat southward. A portion of the forces, less than a third gave chase then paused as the first line vanished only to give chase again when the second line attacked. No lethal force was being used Several ranks kept drawing them southward, but the greater portion of the enemy force stayed at their central location.

The northern flank started the same strategy and forces pursued, but better then half the force remained in the middle and started moving inland. Rengelaqk signaled his forces, they vanished and charged into the enemy ranks, causing minor injuries at random running on through to the water's edge and vanishing again. They caused confusion in the ranks turning to fight them and pulling the Deamorg back in on themselves, effectively stopping their forward movement.

The Deamorg forces that had split off to the north and south suddenly broke off pursuit and headed back to the central force and they all turned in the direction of Shadowkeep ignoring the antagonizing attacks designed to draw attention. The Dark Elf forces found they did not even need to run or vanish; they were just ignored. It was time to step up their methods so far, they had only cause less than a ten hour delay.

Rengelaqk signaled and they vanished again. Injuries were crippling this time. The first two ranks of Deamorg following their leaders collapse to the ground, effectively bringing the forces to a halt again. The elves vanished immediately after the strike. The Daemorg reformed, leaving the fallen on the ground and even they did what they could to drag themselves in pursuit towards Shadow Keep. After the third wave of attacks the Deamorg started taking three steps then doing a massive stop. This caught the Dark Elf forces off guard the first time, there were several injuries, but nobody actually put out of commission. This stopped the Dark Elf penetration of ranks.

They had to change approach again, although this was slowing the Deamorg down sufficiently. There were two reasons to continue pursuit: First if they stopped attacking, the enemy would realize the intent to delay was their objective; Second the more they crippled out of the attacking ranks, the less they would have to fight if they were unsuccessful in removing the mind control.

*   *   *   *   *

Lord Valdir fought against the enemy controlling his actions and every once in a while, he would succeed in making a move that was according to his own will. They had reached the coastline and were being formed up in ranks. He saw a portion of their ranks take off in a southern direction he did not know why. Then another portion headed to the north, he could see no better what they were doing, but hoped it was not successful in serving their new dark master. He saw the Dark Elf attack and immediately realized they were not attempting to kill them, only distract them. This had to be the work of Darval. He tried to call out, but his mind was blocked.

He was able to influence his actions enough to make sure he missed when he swung at their attackers. A subtle twitch and miss. He smiled inwardly when he saw his ranks were all missing. If most were missing, he could give the Dark Elf forces credit, but all missing meant he was not alone in resisting being controlled. The game shifted and with each move it became clearer that whoever was controlling them did not care about their lives, but the Dark Elves were deliberately not killing them. Still, this would mean that Darval was also defending Shadow Keep from their attack or the dark elves now served a different Ancient.

For now, none of that mattered, they needed to stop, they needed to gain control, before they were thrown against the anvil of ShadowKeep as fodder for someone else' war. Lord Valdir almost gained control and then the strength of the control increased. He could feel the change, the necromancer controlling them had dropped control of the fallen so he could re-enforce the control over those who were still of use.

*   *   *   *   *

ShadowDancer saw the change in the fallen Deamorg and heard their plea to the Ancients. She watched the dark elves checking the fallen Deamorg and doing some healing to keep their wounds from going fetal. She reported back the events and whispered to the fallen that help would be there, but the war had to be stopped first.

*   *   *   *   *

The horsemen returned first, the armies of the southern Kingdoms had gone home, divided, morale broken, and supplies diminished. They received a cheer on their success. They quickly joined forces with the defenses or Shadow Keep. Anticipation was not a friend to sleep, and irritability was increasing. Scuffles started breaking out. Bonnie sent out healing waves restoring and compensating for the lack of sleep and the arguing and fighting slowed.

HonorLord and the armies that fought against the undead returned next, another victory. They gave word that the Beast army was maybe two days behind them. From what they had seen, the beasts were as savage to each other as to anything around them. Instincts to fight each other could not be stopped by the mind control, it was apparent the necromantic control required some degree of intellect to be really effective. Finally, the Dark Elves started making their return. From the tower above the gate, HonorLord could see in the distance maybe a day away still the beginnings of the Deamorg army.

"We have the cure," Shiheel said stepping from the light that carried him in. everyone in the war room turned to him. "Where is Hans? It needs to be delivered in airborne form."

"Do you have it with you?" ShadowDancer stepped from the shadows.

"I only have this sample; they are still making more back at the lab and will send it as they get it."

ShadowDancer grabbed the sample without asking, waved her hand and a large jug appeared. Shiheel stepped back. "We need it now." She replied as she filled the jug from the tiny vile and started on the next. A copy of ShadowDancer appeared and vanished with the first jug. "Any ideas on how to make it airborne?"

"Just vaporize it and use mage wind to deliver it."

"I need to get it to the fallen Deamorg so that they can be healed quickly." She finished another jug, "Take this to HonorLord. I have a visual on Jaharadan." She called into the air as if she could see them, Darval, Gaharias."

The two materialized in the room. "You summoned us?" Gaharias stammered with surprise.

"You, Gaharias, have had your hands tied as to what you can do, you would not be allowed to control an army or force events like this correct?"

He looked around a little uncomfortable discussing the issue in front of non-Ancients, "Where are you going with this?"

"Why don't we just have Jaharadan sign the accord and become an Ancient?"

They looked at her like she was crazy, "He would be an Ancient then," Darval started, "and then," understanding clicked in, "he will have no more power than he does, but he will not be allowed to act directly in the affairs of this world.

ShadowDancer sent out three more jugs of the potion filled two more and set the vile down, "Get the accord for him to sign and the required witnesses. I will bring him when you are ready, I don't want him to have time to think about it."

*   *   *   *   *

Hans held the jug of green fluid; he estimated the jug to be about a gallon and a half. He watched as the fog formed in front or the ground troops below. The gap was closing as the Deamorg approached. The mages cast and the fog moved forward. The giant race moved into the fog; the leader raised his staff swinging down. At the last second the swing lurched to the side and the thundering boom hit the dirt causing a cloud of brown to burst upwards.

A cheer went up from the armies. Archer and casters stayed at the ready, but with held their release. The leader of the Deamorg army let out a shrieking roar that sent a chill though every soul. Something closing in from the West answered. The thundering approach of the beast army could be heard. Hans began pouring the bottle in the air in front of him, vaporizing it as it came out of the bottle sending it streaming in the direction the beasts would be arriving from.

Lord Valdir now in control followed in the same direction. As the first beast bounded out of the green fog he roared and the creatures coming out of the fog cowered before him and vanished in the direction from whence they came.

"Thank you, Lord Valdir." Hans projected his thoughts to the beast. *"Darval has come for you to take you to the shadow realm if you choose to go with him. If you choose to stay, I am sure we can offer you a home on the northern cliffs."*

Lord Valdir turned towards ShadowKeep, *"My thanks Ancient of War my people will make their own choices. Those who stay may accept your offer."*

*   *   *   *   *

They were gathered in the royal hall of ShadowKeep, the council of Ancients in their places, one of the old ones presided at the end of the table, when asked his name he simply said, "Not important."

"Bring him now." Gaharias stated.

ShadowDancer brought Jaharadan to the end of the table opposite from the Old One and kept his assistant, Jahaln back in the cave. "Welcome, Jaharadan." no emotion showed in her voice.

"What?!" He looked around quickly.

"You sought to be an Ancient, sign the accord and be one of us." Gaharais said deliberately inflecting disappointment.

He looked at Darval, "You have chosen to sponsor me?" a touch of victory sounded in his voice.

"Actually, it is by ShadowDancer's choice you live." Darval scoffed as if he were dismissing a bug that deserved less than his attention.

He looked at the female Ancient he had never seen before. He could not read her, or place where she fit in the puzzle, "My gratitude."

"Sign before I change my mind." her voice had so much disinterest it haunted her, "The council of elders is here to witness your ascension as is the witness of the Old Ones we cannot keep their time all day. Unless of course you are waiting for opposition to our actions to arrive?"

He turned quickly and signed the accord, no sense inviting an opportunity to oppose his becoming an Ancient, "Done." He smiled pleased with his success.

The Old One spoke, "It is done, you have signed the accord and are counted among the Ancients of Ethar and are bound as they are to the rules and freedoms of the accord."

Another Ancient appeared with urgency in his eyes, "Don't sign Jaharadan!"

"You are too late to stop his membership, Nuas." the old one stated, "It is done." The accord leaped into the hands of the Old One.

Nuas was obviously angered, "Fool, did you not read before you signed? We were given no choice at the time of the accord, but you were accepted as an Ancient in order to be offered the chance to sign. Now you cannot act directly in the affairs of Ethar and you must let the people make their choices. You can only act through you followers."

Jaharadan knew he was trapped, but he still had an ace up his sleeve, "I am not without my means. I have one powerful enough to act as my Avatar."

ShadowDancer summoned Jahaln, "Meet my servant who came to me of his own will."

Jaharadan internalized his rage, he had been betrayed. *I have others, perhaps not as powerful, but they will learn in time.* He looked at ShadowDancer, "You have tricked me and won this time witch, but there will be times to come."

"Would you preferred I had not spared your life and perhaps made you to serve me instead?" her voice was filled with venom now, "It was my choice, and I can still change my mind."

"She is not bound by the accord." the Old One pointed out. "there are others not bound." his glance included those present who were not bound, including Darval.

Jaharadan knew any one of them could have eliminated him from the game and had second thoughts about being angry at ShadowDancer, he bowed slightly to ShadowDancer, "Perhaps I need to learn the new rules of the game before I speak rashly." He vanished, but they all knew where he was as they could sense any Ancients unless they shielded their presence. ShadowDancer as his sponsor would always be able to locate him now, even if he was hiding from the rest.

"We are all wise and foolish at the same time." the Old One was transforming back into dragon form as he vanished.

HonorLord stepped to the head of the table, "It is done. This war is over. We have much to clean up. I thank all who have extended themselves to assist."

"I think we have new protectors of Ethar." Darval stated, "Once I have all those who choose to follow me to the shadow realms, I may be finding myself signing that accord. I can still answer those who call, but this world no longer needs me."

"I think you should wait." ShadowDancer said, "It is not time yet."

"What do you mean?" Gaharias stepped towards ShadowDancer

"Ethar is changing, and destiny is setting the threads in place." ShadowDancer was glowing more than usual her eyes somewhat distant, "Your destiny is elsewhere, but you must have free course until my time has come and I still have much to learn. You are one of my teachers." The glowing subdued.

Darval pondered a moment, "The last prophet among the ancients wrote the never-ending poem, then scattered it in pieces throughout the world never to be restored to its fullness. Our daughter of destiny has been touched by the threads of time."

"She has also summoned three Ancients without their consent, You, me and Jaharadan. That is a power only the old ones possessed. I suspect her father is as powerful, perhaps more, but his destiny also is divided." Gaharias paused, "I suspect that even the old ones are preparing to move on to other things."

The others stayed silent. ShadowDancer saw all eyes were on her. "Please let this pass. I was caught up in what I was seeing." One more thing I need to learn to bring under control and I have yet to perfect being in more than one place at a time. The thought reminded her and with another thought Chareece was standing in her bedroom, checking her clothing and heading out to see her parents.

"Eric, Bonny, would you mind doing me a favor?" HonorLord inquired.

"Anything." Eric answered, bonny frowned at his haste.

"All of those beasts need to be sent back to their homes and there may be a lot of healing and repairing that need to be done in their wake."

"We'll take care of it." Bonny patted him on the shoulder. They conferred for a moment and vanished.

ShadowDancer pulled Gaharias to the side. "There was an elf village on this continent. They had an adoma. They were destroyed save for one child. Where they yours?"

Gaharias looked very troubled, "They were hidden. They should have been safe."

"An undead army does not have to see what is in its path to destroy it."

"Where is the child, what was the name?" Gaharias was genuinely concerned.

"Okay, I will not beat you up over this, I think you will do that well enough yourself. Her name was Leleshi and she is in a place where she will be safe. She is neither on Ethar, nor on earth."

"Please keep her safe, she was the child of the shane, leader of their tribe. I have said I have a remnant of my people on every continent. They were my remnant on this continent, and I thought they were safe. They never called to me."

"They probably thought they were safe also, until it was too late. Why didn't you tell me the place we build in our minds is an entire new dimension? A plain of existence where we can build planets and stars and," she stopped, the expression on Gaharias face said this too was something he did not know before.

"Perhaps it is better not to tell anyone else about this? Imagine what someone who likes to build armies might do with that knowledge?" Gaharias seemed to be pleading with her.

"What knowledge" Darval asked as he stepped over.

"Nothing really." Gaharias said, "Just discussing some of the finer nuances of our abilities. Like you and your Dark Elf warriors, a card that was not seen until after the game was in motion."

"Ah yes, it was never my intent for them to ever return. Now that they are here however, they are helping me find my followers that wish to move over to the new realm and those that wish to stay." Darval turned to ShadowDancer, "And you! You seem to have won the hearts of a portions of my races. Take good care of them, if they follow you, they are yours."

*   *   *   *   *

Only a small contingent of the Deamorg actually made up of two races, a vampire-like race and a gargoyle-like race, decided to stay. HonorLord kept his word and they marked out a territory in the rocky north eastern part of the continent to make their home. Help would be provided to make their dwelling and move any belongings they wanted from the forbidden lands. The southern kingdoms and baronies were more than willing to concede to open trade and paying ShadowKeep 10% of their next year's taxes as restitution for their willing support of an enemy of ShadowKeep.

"It is good having you here," Hans said to Bonnie and Eric. "You do not have to wait for a war to visit."

"We won't wait, we will make a point of driving you crazy with too many visits." Bonnie smiled, "The statue you made by the inner gates overlooking the village is wonderful, and a reminder of what Stralina did for the people."

Hans looked almost embarrassed, "I know it may seem soon, but I may have someone for you to meet sooner than I would have expected."

"Don't forget, you have an obligation to be at our earth wedding. Perhaps you can introduce us there?" Eric was glad to see Hans was going to be alright, "And Jaffro owes me a term-paper." he laughed.

*   *   *   *   *

ShadowDancer gently touched the side of Melina's head. Everything she had seen and done passed through. She let go of most of what was private between Melina and her sister. "I am glad you care enough for your sister to be willing to sacrifice your relationship for the good of her health. I think I can send her on a vision that will resolve that issue so that you will not have to." she pulled her hand back, "I did give much more in that gift then I intended. Moving forward, my people can keep those things they have already discovered that they can do but will not automatically be able to do the rest. Their abilities may grow as they earn favor and new followers will have to earn their way, beyond being able to harvest what they need to survive."

"What about my sisters' shrine and secret stash?"

"I love the statue. And she was Wise in her actions, I will not undo what is done."

Chareece filled her mom and dad, the king and queen in on what she felt they should know. They were glad to have her back and did not pry about her alter ego. Talmorg did pull out a gold coin, "This showed up in a shop in town. The merchant didn't recognize the coin, so he exchanged it with a guard at the palace gate and it was brought to me."

Chareece took the coin, looked at it and smile, "I think this is mine." She slipped the coin into a pocket, "They will keep their coins of honorable weight, if not generous."

*   *   *   *   *

Eric and Bonny Paid Talmorg and Saphrine a visit before returning to earth.

"So, when it came down to final events, ShadowDancer grabbed control and made the decisions that saved the day." Eric was explaining over dinner as they ate.

Talmorg nodded, and glanced at Chareece, "It is good to know we are at peace again, but this is a good warning not to become overconfident. We need to be prepared for unexpected hostilities."

"Not so prepared that we make them happen though." Saphrine added.

"We are going to have a wedding ceremony on earth soon, they do not recognize our marriage here. I wish we could bring you there to attend, but we could not possibly uproot you from here and customs and manners are so different you may not be comfortable." Eric stated.

"Yes," Bonny added, "It will be official in both worlds."

"I could represent our family." Chareece offered, "and nobody would need to know I was gone."

"That would be up to Eric and Bonny." Talmorg looked at them, Saphrine nodded her agreement.

"You would be welcome." Bonny smiled, "But you have to keep in mind we are not known there the same as we are known here. Perhaps you might join us with time to become more familiar with the ways of our world and we could help you avoid any pitfalls."

Chareece thought about the things she had already done and wondered how much trouble she already caused. They did not have to know everything she had done; be she was going to have to bring her father in on some things. "It will be an honor to learn the proper boundaries in your world."

Discussion moved to the issues of the kingdom. They discuss the rebuilding that was going on. Relationships between the races and mixed races came up and their neighbors to the west in the dwarfish kingdom. Agreements for open trading were being reached and the crack in the world formed a barrier to those arrangements. A ferrying service could be set up at the coast, but the restriction would limit trade only to those items that were worth the cost. They were going to have to find ways to bridge the chasm in many places to effectively open relations across the border with Darkolan.

Eric suggested that perhaps he could provide some bridge designs form earth that they could offer to the dwarf engineers that they might be able to use for building bridges of metal and stone. It was suggesting that they may need to collaborate with gnomes to accomplish that task.

They bid their farewells and when they were out of her parents' sight, Chareece became two one staying in the palace and the other going with Eric and Bonny back to earth. They would tell Bonny's mom she was from Eric's side of the family, well, she actually was.

*   *   *   *   *

Eric sat in quiet contemplation. Even if he was a descendant of Gaharias Emarlandestria, even if he had the power to bend the fabric of the multi-verse he had come to know, he did not think of himself as a "god". His upbringing had been lax when it came to religious matters, but he was still convinced that there was one God. He was convinced that it was the same God no matter who or where you came from. When he answered the petitions of the peoples of Ethar he always tried to do what he considered to be right and hoped it was in service to what was true. If he was given this great power, there had to be a reason and with it a responsibility. Perhaps this was all part of the evolutionary process of mankind, in the broader sense of all the races of course.

He broke away from his identity crisis and answered Bonnie's question, "Sure, why wouldn't we go to your mom's place for Thanksgiving dinner." He smiled warmly into her eye. "Besides, I don't think she would have it any other way since her miraculous recovery in the hospital the first time we came back."

"It definitely surprised the doctors, as a matter of fact, it has been over a year and they still won't stop running tests on her to try and figure out what happened." The twinge of irritation came and went from her brow. "Perhaps we should have healed everyone in the hospital that day when we came back just to take some of the attention off of her.

Eric's eyes went distant for but a flash of a moment, "The random healing throughout the city did draw some of the attention off. I am glad Chareece came forward with what happened when she did. I still have not come to terms with the limits of what we can or should do here on earth. I don't even know what rules we should or should not follow on Ethar."

"And you spend too much time thinking about it too. When I am moved, I heal. I am just careful not to do anything ostentatious here on earth that might draw attention to what we can do." Bonnie glanced out the window at house of Jaffro Jaimes and the black van that was always parked across the street keeping him under surveillance. "Look at how they watch Jaimes and all he did was disappear for a few months and bring back a few artifacts."

"We could stop them." Eric snickered, "But it is entertaining seeing them out there every day with all that high-tech equipment monitoring his house and following him all over the world."

Putting the last of the dishes away in the cupboard, "That was a good move on his part to become a world explorer and archaeologist as a cover for what happened."

"That and look at all he has learned and shared with us since he started his explorations." They both went silent thinking about the historical interactions between the worlds they lived in. "I don't think it is all just a cover. He has done some very thorough research on ancient gods and goddesses. I suspect he is trying to get a better grip on what we are."

"And how are my newlyweds doing." Bes asked letting herself in the front door.

"It has been months," Eric protested with a laugh

"First year, still newlyweds. Don't you ever check your mail?" she dropped a stack of envelopes on the table, "Do you know an agent Dawson with the FBI?" she gave the large envelope one more flip before handing it to Eric.

Some define good and evil by their own beliefs, to the extent you agree with them you are good, wherever you disagree you are evil. Others define it by intent. The one sure thing about sentient beings and good and evil it is defined by the perspective of the individual proclaiming their concept and pushed on those who do not refute the claim. In the end in a society the laws declare good and evil by those who have the power or support to enforce them. When forces considered dark and evil by enough of the population of a society have been making the laws for that society for enough time forces will explode and there will be a re-balancing of what is defined as good and evil. Contrarily when a population has been given the opportunity to have a free social order with open tolerance for varied concepts, darker elements of the society will attempt to creep into place trying to force their concepts of good and evil and choke out the freedom of others around them. If we were to all call after the same God and believe that that God gave us the freedom to choose, we would stand up against those who would take that choice away and defend the rights of those who may not agree with us, knowing that allowing laws to declare good and evil can lead to laws against our own practice of what we believe is good. You cannot have freedom to follow after your beliefs of good and evil without allowing the freedom to those who believe contrary to our own beliefs.